Lilac
in
Scarlet

CHRISTINE DORAN

ISBN-10: 1544191634

ISBN-13: 978-1544191638

Also by Christine Doran:

Lilac in Black and White

GLOSSARY FOR NON-IRISH READERS

If you're not from Ireland you might not be familiar with some of the words and phrases Lilac uses, so I've included a glossary to help you out.

Spellings and punctuation in this book are in British-English style, so they might look a little unfamiliar to American readers. They're not wrong (except in the letters, when Lilac and Margery need to pay more attention to their spelling).

biccie	short for biscuit
biscuit	cookie
bobbin	hair elastic
boot	trunk (of a car)
Club Milk	a small chocolate bar
dote	cute small child or baby
fifth class	fifth grade
fish fingers	fish sticks
give out to	scold, tell off
Guard, Garda	policeman or woman (plural is Gardaí)
jumper	sweater
junior infants	equivalent of kindergarten or pre-k
lead	leash

Modh Coinníollach	conditional mood (Irish grammar)
nick	to steal
plait	braid
the pledge	a promise not to drink alcohol until you're 18
puke	vomit
rucksack	backpack
runners	sneakers
Sellotape	sticky tape, Scotch tape
shuttlecock	birdie (badminton)
stone (weight)	1 stone is 14 lbs or 6.3 kilos
swimming togs	swimsuit
train tracks	braces (on teeth)
tenner	ten-pound note (money)

Once upon a time, a little girl grew up in a tall, narrow house by the sea, with a father who painted pictures and a mother who wrote books, and a big dog who jumped up and down all day. The girl had fat yellow curls that tangled into a thicket every night in bed, and pink cheeks, and big solemn eyes that looked out at the world. Her name was Lilac.

CHAPTER 1

There was a girl on the beach, throwing pieces of driftwood into the sea for her dog to run after. The girl had blondish-brownish curls that blew into her face and the dog was a big bounding thing that was going to shake his wet fur all over her any minute now. He did, and she shrieked and laughed, and he gambolled over to her feet and instantly away again in excitement. The weather was mild, the sun shining and the breeze not cutting – but the seawater held a deep chill, because only the most optimistic would ever call the Irish Sea warm. And it was March, after all.

They looked bound together, a unit: the girl and the dog.

The dog scrabbled in the shingle, after a scent. He dug up a piece of rag and tossed it towards the girl, looking proud of his find. She was not impressed. He went back to the same spot and investigated further, snuffling down into the wet stony sand, worrying at something with a paw. The girl went over to him.

'What have you found, Guzzler? What is it, boy?' she asked. 'It's probably just a dirty old piece of rubbish, leave it alone. Here, get the stick.' She waved her piece of driftwood and threw it for him, off towards the water on the other side. He ran. She peered into the hole he had dug and saw a shiny corner of something. She poked it with her toe and wiggled it until it came loose. Then she bent down and reached into the sand to pull it out.

It was a box. A small, tarnished, metal box with hinges and a lid with a pattern. Lilac – that was the girl's name, though she didn't like it much – tried to flip the lid open, but it was stuck because one corner had been dented. It was definitely A Find, though, the sort you didn't come across every day. She took a mostly clean hanky out of her jeans pocket and wiped the sand and damp off the metal. It felt very smooth, except for the dent. It looked almost black, but she could tell that it would polish up to something shinier with some of the polish she used to use on Granny's candlesticks, if they had any of that at home.

Lilac wrapped the box carefully in her hanky and put it in her small rucksack, which held her wallet (containing one pound fifty), her pencil case (containing two pencils, a green crayon, and a ruler), and a pair of mittens she didn't need. She liked the important feeling of carrying a bag of some sort, but she never knew what to put in it, because she didn't really need to bring anything with her when she went down to the beach with Guzzler. But here was something to carry and she was glad she'd brought the bag.

She picked up a shiny black stone, warm from the sun, and closed her fingers over it, absorbing its smooth heat. A vein of white ran through its centre, and she thought if she had a chisel she could break it open and see the white layer all the way down, something nobody on earth had ever seen before. Instead, she brought her arm back and threw it as far into the sea as she could. There would always be another stone. The beach was full of them, coming and going, rolling over each other with the tide and the winter storms and the summer ripples.

She called Guzzler and set off for home, knowing he would be behind her in a minute, like a slippery shadow. The stones got bigger as you came to the top of the beach, so that first they rolled away under your feet and then they stayed still while you picked your way from one to another. The biggest ones at the top were enclosed in wire in huge blocks like giants' bricks, to form a barrier that couldn't be taken away by even the strongest storms, so that the coastline would stay where it was put and not move up to bring the road into the sea, and then the whole town. At least, that was what her father said. He remembered when the cliffs went out further, when there were houses on the sea side of the road further up the coast, where there are no houses now because they're in the sea. The sea eats everything in the end, he said.

Well, Lilac thought, sometimes it pukes things up, too. It puked me up an interesting box and I'm going to polish it and see what's inside it. Or keep things in it, if it's empty. It hadn't made a noise when she'd shaken it, so if there was something inside, it didn't rattle. And it didn't seem particularly heavy, so it probably didn't hold gold coins or diamonds or rubies. But you never know, she thought.

'Mum! What do you polish things with?' Lilac shouted as she took her windcheater off and unclipped Guzzler's lead from his collar. Lilac's mother came out of the kitchen and leaned against the door frame, licking a wooden spoon thoughtfully. She was tall and somehow always elegant, even wearing an old skirt and a blouse with tomatoey splashes on it.

She held out the implement, a hand cupped underneath to catch any drips. 'Taste this and tell me if it needs more salt. Or maybe more tomato. Polish what sort of things? We have Pledge, for polishing the dining-room table.' Lilac looked doubtfully at the wooden spoon, which was coated with a dark brown sauce, and took a sniff.

'Is that chocolate? For polishing metal, I mean. I found this at the beach, look.' She rummaged in her rucksack and pulled out her find.

'No, of course it's not chocolate, Lilac. It's spaghetti bolognese. At least, it's the bolognese part. We don't have any spaghetti so we're having it with potatoes. That's very nice,' she added, looking at the box Lilac was waving under her nose. 'Try some Silvo. I think there might be some under the stairs. I used to use it on the good photo frames. You could have a go at those too, while you're at it.'

Lilac rooted through the various containers of ancient cleaning fluids and goos that lived in the crate in the under-the-stairs wonderland, her progress hampered by the semi-darkness because the light bulb had gone out again. Finally, she dragged the whole thing out into the hall and took out the mostly empty bottles and tubs one by one, until she came to a tin that looked more like shoe polish than anything else, but said 'Silvo' in big, bold, circus-like lettering. Then she put everything else back in again and pushed the crate back to where it had been, more or less.

She found a rag in the bag that hung on the back of the door. The lid twisted stiffly open to reveal surprisingly pink gunk – she scooped out a blob and started to rub it onto the metal box. She sat down on the dark wooden hall floor, concentrating hard on her job. Within a few minutes, the box had started to come up beautifully silver, and Lilac's hands and her jumper were blackish in patches. She worked away until all the dark tarnish was gone, even between the bumps of the swirls on the lid and the beading along the edges, and then she took it into the kitchen to show it off.

'Oh, that's lovely, Lilac. Give it a wipe with a damp cloth to get the stuff off. And wash your hands,' her mother added, noticing that the tarnish was now all over Lilac instead.

It really was lovely. Almost white in its silverness, it looked brand new now, apart from the dent in the corner. The smooth underside, if she held it close enough, reflected Lilac's face back at her: round cheeks, messy curls, freckles on the bridge of her nose, and dark blue eyes. When she moved it away everything went wibbly-wobbly, like a fun-house mirror or looking in the back of a spoon. The top, with the pattern, didn't work so well as a mirror. There were some tiny marks stamped in the bottom: a lion, an anchor, the letter F. It was like a secret code. Lilac was delighted.

She still couldn't open the lid, so she put the box away in her bedroom until she could ask her dad for help with it.

CHAPTER 2

Easter was coming up. So was Lilac's birthday (she'd be eleven), and so was her Confirmation. Just like buses, everything comes at once, her granny said when Lilac told her about it on the phone. Granny was going to try to visit from Cork for the birthday and the Confirmation, if she didn't have an exhibition that weekend. Granny had taken up watercolours after she moved from Dublin to Cork, and seemed to be having a bit of success with them.

Lilac's class had to have decided on their Confirmation names by Monday. Lilac had a lot of names under consideration. Choosing a new name was the best thing about getting confirmed, really, since Confirmation didn't mean you were able to do anything new the way First Confession and First Communion had. (Getting the Holy Spirit didn't count, since the flaming tongue – or was it a tongue of flame? – didn't show up in real life.) And you didn't get a special dress like at First Communion either; in fact, they would have to wear their uniforms, which seemed all wrong after the pomp of Communion dresses when she had been only seven and so much less able to appreciate a dress. Lilac knew very well that everyone in her class would get a new outfit to wear out to lunch afterwards anyway, so there was no point saying it saved money.

Lilac took her Confirmation Name Ideas list down from her pinboard. Some people said it had to be a saint's name, but Lilac hadn't heard the priest say that specifically. And she didn't see how you could prove that there hadn't been a very good person named any name at all, so she had put all the names she wished she was called on the list, at least to start with. It looked like this:

Angelina

Felicity

Shrove

Etáin

Lucy

Robinette

Claudine

Veronica

She added 'Heavenly', which was a beautiful name and also sounded very holy, so she thought it would be perfect for Confirmation.

Lilac already had two middle names – Adelaide and Philomena – so there wasn't likely to be much space for another on any forms she might ever fill out. She was hoping, actually, that she might be able to replace

Philomena with her new name, at least unofficially. But she was afraid she'd always feel the need to explain that, which would probably make it not worthwhile. She really needed to discuss this with someone; it wasn't the sort of important decision she could make alone.

Lilac went back downstairs, hoping to ring her friend Agatha. Ringing friends was still a bit of a new departure for Lilac, but she thought this would be a good reason to do it. Except now her mother was on the phone, and judging by the nodding and 'mm-hmmm'-ing, it would be a long one. Probably Eileen McGrath, mother of Jeannie-the-babysitter, Lilac thought knowingly. Eileen would talk the hind leg off a donkey, her mother always said when she would finally put down the phone and flex her wrist and rub the back of her neck, as if they were stiff from holding it for so long. And yet there she'd be the next time, nodding and mm-hmming away all over again.

Lilac looked out the bay window of the front room and craned her neck to see as far up the street as she could. She guessed that Michael Jennings was bouncing a tennis ball against the door of his garage; she couldn't see him, but she could hear the bang of fuzzy green on metal at regular intervals. She made a few exaggerated gestures to let her mother know that she was going outside – probably much more distracting than just saying so, judging by her mother's impatient hand-flapping in response – and ran outside and up the road in her socks, list of names in hand. It was dry underfoot, and she'd left her shoes in her bedroom.

'Hi, Michael,' she said, suddenly a little shy. She and Michael had got to know each other a bit in the past few months, but she still needed a reason to go and talk to him, she couldn't just call down to his house to hang around the way she could with Agatha or her other friend Margery. (Margery had gone to live in Canada for a year, but last summer she and Lilac had been in and out of each other's houses all the time.)

'Hi. Do you want to play sevens?'

'Not really. I need help choosing my Confirmation name. Have you chosen yours?' The boys' school would be making their Confirmations at the same time, so that the bishop only had to come down from Dublin once. He was a busy man, the bishop, especially at this time of year with all the Confirmations.

'No. No, I haven't.' Michael answered very quickly, looking a bit red under his freckles. His curly brown hair was wiggling into his eyes and he kept brushing it out.

'Oh. Well, I have a list and I need to decide by tomorrow. Listen and tell me which sounds best.' She gabbled off the names on the list.

'Wait, wait.' Michael stopped bouncing the tennis ball and sat on his front doorstep. 'Show me the list. I can't keep them all in my head. Why have you no shoes on?'

'I just . . . don't. I was in a hurry.' Lilac sat down beside him and held out her list so they could both read it. Standing up she was a tiny bit taller than Michael, but sitting down his head was higher than hers.

'Is Shrove a name?' Michael asked.

'Definitely.'

'OK.' He didn't sound convinced. 'I think . . . I like Lucy. It's sort of, well, normal.'

'I know. And you'd think with being called Lilac I'd want

something normal, wouldn't you?'

'That's not what I meant. I mean, I didn't . . . Lilac's a nice name. It suits you.'

'Thank you, but I wish it didn't,' she said quickly. She always said that, because people always said it suited her. They had to, because she was always the only Lilac anyone had ever met. 'But anyway. Sometimes I want normal, and sometimes I want unusual that I get to choose for myself. I can't decide. That's why I need help.'

'Well, have you thought about what your initials will spell? You could make a cool word. Or you could make sure you don't accidentally give yourself initials that spell something bad.'

'Ooh, good point.' Lilac was impressed. 'Well, my initials now are L-A-P-M. That doesn't spell anything. Without Philomena – because I pretend it's not there sometimes – they'd be L-A-M.'

They tried without success to make words by putting random letters in before the M, but nothing worked. Then they tried anagrams, by moving the initials around.

'You could be CLAM if you chose Claudine and dropped the Philomena. Or MAPLE if you took Etáin. Or PHLAM, is that a word?'

'It sounds like a word, maybe. My mum knew someone who took Sivle for her Confirmation name. The bishop wasn't sure it was allowed but she said it was an ancient saint from Roman times. It was actually "Elvis" backwards, because she really liked Elvis.'

'Do you want to do that? Wait, is Shrove something backwards? Evorhs – no. Hovers. Horse V . . . Rovesh . . . am I close? Am I getting somewhere?' He was grinning, and she knew he was just teasing her.

'No, it's just Shrove, honestly. I think it's pretty. There's a song about Ruby Tuesday, and then there's Shrove Tuesday, and so I think that should be a name too.'

'How about Ruby?'

'Nah, it's too much like Lilac. I mean, it's a colour, and part of nature as well. I like it for other people, just not for me.' She thought for a second. 'Can I have the pen?' He handed her the blue biro he'd been using to make the anagrams. Its lid was a bit chewed, so she tried not to touch that part.

'Not Felicity, because of the F sound beside Philomena. And it's too long. Which also takes out Veronica and Angelina. And Robinette,' she added, striking it out with a sigh. 'I really liked that one.'

'But it's nature as well,' Michael pointed out. 'It might make people think about robins in lilac bushes.' He carefully didn't say that he himself would think that, which Lilac appreciated.

'Ugh. I've gone off it suddenly. We're left with Shrove, Etáin, Lucy and Claudine.'

'You could take out Lucy because you already have an L name,' Michael suggested, nobly sacrificing his first choice because he knew she didn't like it as much as he did, but she felt bad about taking it off the list while he was there.

'Etáin is really nice, but people in other countries wouldn't know how to pronounce it. What if I live in Australia and I'm famous and people are always mispronouncing my name?' Michael nodded solemnly. 'That would never do. I think it has to go.' She loved all the names, but there was a certain satisfaction about crossing things off and whittling down the choice to just two.

'Now all you have to do is sleep on it and you'll know in the morning,' Michael declared with certainty. 'That's what I always do.'

'Will I dream the answer?'

'You might.'

They both paused. The job was done, and they had nothing left to talk about.

'I should go, then. Thanks for your help. I'd never have thought of the initials thing on my own.'

'Sure. See you.'

'See you.'

CHAPTER 3

Lilac's socks were black on the bottom when she got back to the house. She put them in the laundry basket before anyone noticed, and went upstairs to start a letter to Margery. Even though Margery had been gone since last August, they still wrote to each other quite faithfully. Sometimes it felt a little too much as if Margery was a diary instead of a real girl temporarily in another country. Lilac wasn't entirely sure how they'd fit together again as real-life friends when she came back.

Dear Margery,
[the letter said]
    I have to have decided on my Confirmation name by tomorrow. I am down to two options. I'm not going to tell you what they are in case you pick the wrong one because by the time you tell me which you prefer it'll be too late. I'm going to sleep on it and decide in the morning. At first I

thought I'd just wait and see if I dreamed about the names, but actually I'm going to really sleep on them. I'll write the two names on pieces of paper and I'll put them under my pillow as if I'm waiting for the tooth fairy, and in the morning if one is still there and the other has fallen down, or one is right in the middle and the other is off to one side, that will be A Sign and I'll know which one to pick.

Lilac knew Michael hadn't meant her to take his suggestion literally, but she liked this plan. She cut two pieces of paper exactly the same size and wrote 'Claudine' on one and 'Shrove' on the other and decorated them with flowers and little bluebirds, and a few tongues of fire to make it holy, and put them right in the middle of the pillow area. She considered saying a little prayer asking God to guide her to the right choice, but then she decided God probably had more important things to be thinking about than that, and she didn't want to bother Him.

Then she went back to the letter and finished it off with some updates on school and weather.

When she went to bed that night, it was hard to get to sleep. Lilac normally slept on her side, curled up like a question mark, with one hand under her pillow. But every time she started to slip her hand into its usual place, she was afraid she'd move the paper, so she would try to find somewhere else for the hand to go. She fell asleep eventually, but she kept dreaming that she was awake, and that her pillow was being moved by some invisible force, or that it was morning and all the paper had disappeared, along with most of her bedroom walls. It was not a restful night.

When her mother called up the stairs in the morning – 'Lilac! Aren't you up yet?' – Lilac was finally deep, deep down at the bottom of a well of sleep. She felt herself swimming up through thick layers of consciousness, unwilling, into daylight. Her arms and legs were velcroed to the mattress. She didn't want to move. Slowly, she remembered the two pieces of paper under her pillow. She sat up and carefully lifted the pillow straight up into the air, to preserve the scene exactly as it was. One scrap of paper was right there; the other was nowhere to be seen.

'It's A Sign!' Lilac exclaimed. She picked up the paper and turned it over. Claudine. 'Oh.' She went downstairs. 'Mum?'

'You'd better hurry, Lilac. You're going to be late, look at the time. What is it?'

'I thought I liked two things exactly the same amount, but now it turns out I liked one better all along. Am I allowed do the opposite of what I was going to do?'

'What? Yes. Yes, of course you are. Unless it's a bad thing.'

'Mum, you're just saying what you think I want you to say, so I'll hurry up and go to school.'

'Yes, you're right. Please hurry up and go to school.'

'But I have to know *before* I go to school. We have to have decided today.'

'Let me get this straight, then. You have to make a choice, and you were going to do one thing but now you want to do the other?'

'Yes.'

'Well, it sounds perfectly reasonable to change your mind.'

'Good. Can I open the new variety pack of cereals even though I haven't finished the box of Rice Krispies? I *really* want Honey-Nut Cornflakes.'

'Yes, fine, all right, I suppose so.'

Lilac could see that her mother was distracted and trying to rush Lilac out the door so that she could get down to some writing. That was her job, she wrote books. Lilac had never read further than the first few pages of her mother's books because they were grown-up novels and not all that interesting to Lilac, but she liked looking at the covers and reading the backs – which made them sound more exciting than they really were, her mother said. She wondered what else she could get her mother to agree to while she was in this mood.

'Mum, can I have a pony?'

'Maybe for your birthday,' her mum said without looking up, licking a finger and flicking through a pile of typed-up pages looking for something.

'REALLY? Next *month*?'

'What? Oh. No, not next month, that's all sorted out. Maybe for Christmas, then. Put it on your list. Wait, what did you ask for?' Her mother looked up, belatedly. 'A pony? No! I meant no. Stop it now, eat your breakfast and get dressed, there's no time for this nonsense.'

'Mum, it's raining, Will you give me a lift?'

'If you're ready in ten minutes. Now you've made me lose my place.'

Lilac shovelled the last two spoonfuls of sweet, delicious crunchiness into her mouth, lifted the bowl with both hands to slurp the last of the milk, and took the stairs at a run to get dressed and brush her teeth in record time.

CHAPTER 4

Miss Grey passed out forms on which everyone in fifth class was to fill in their name and address and birth date and the name they were taking for their Confirmation. Lilac happily wrote 'Shrove' in the space for the name she had chosen, and handed it up.

'Lilac, can you come up here? I think there's a mistake,' Miss Grey called out a little later as she sat at her desk checking off all the forms. Lilac's heart sank. She had put so much trouble into narrowing down her list, and she knew she had mocked Fate by deciding The Sign meant she should choose the one she *couldn't* find under her pillow, because that was the one she really wanted, so maybe Fate was now clobbering her for it. She pushed back her chair with a horrible screech of metal on floor tile, winced, and slouched up to the front of the room.

'Lilac, please take more care with your chair. Now, I think you've put in the wrong thing here for your date of birth. The fifteenth of April is the date of the Confirmation Mass.'

'It's my birthday too, Miss Grey. We're going out for a doubly special lunch because it's two special things at once. My granny's taking us all to the Swiss Chalet, for chicken and chips and coleslaw and Coke floats.' The new Swiss Chalet restaurant was the height of sophistication.

'Oh.' Miss Grey smiled benignly. 'Oh, well, that's fine then. I thought you were mixed up, that's all. Maybe I'll put a little note in here to say that it really is your birthday, in case the bishop's staff think the same thing when they check these. You may go back to your seat. And mind that chair.'

With a spring in her step, Lilac returned to her desk and lifted her chair as carefully as ever she could over the floor tiles to make a silent re-entry. Miss Grey hadn't said a word about Shrove, so it must be a perfectly acceptable name. There was probably a Saint Shrove, in the 1700s maybe, in France maybe. She would have been very poor and very beautiful and she wore a flowing blue dress and ministered to the children of the people who were even poorer. The barefoot tots gazed upon Saint Shrove's golden tresses with awe and gratitude as she handed out scones and bananas even though it meant she'd go hungry later that day . . . Lilac spent the next ten minutes happily wrapped in a daydream instead of paying any attention at all to long multiplication.

After break, Miss Grey had an announcement to make. Lilac nudged Agatha and said, 'Maybe she's going to invite us all to her wedding.' Miss Grey was engaged, but she wouldn't tell anyone anything about when she was getting married or who her fiancé was. Lilac and Agatha had spent entire lunchtimes inventing details about him and about the ceremony, and now felt a deeply vested interest in being invited along on the big day. Agatha giggled.

'We have been asked,' Miss Grey said, 'to contribute to the Easter ceremonies in the church. At the Family Mass on Easter Sunday morning, a group from our class will perform an interpretative dance on the altar. It's a great honour, and whoever is chosen must be very reverent, as well as being graceful and expressing themselves elegantly through the music.'

Some barely suppressed vomiting noises came from the back of the room. Miss Grey decided it would be most dignified to ignore them, so she pressed on without comment. 'Sixth Class will sing "Here I Am, Lord" and Miss Taylor will choreograph a simple set of flowing movements to go along with the hymn. We've put together a shortlist of girls for the dance group, but this might change as we see how things work out.'

That evening, Lilac told her mother all about it in injured tones.

'And then, it was *so unfair*, Miss Taylor had been spying on us! In PE yesterday when Mrs Ellis put on "The Lion Sleeps Tonight" and said we could all dance our little hearts out to it – I should have known, because she never says things like that – she was making a list in her head of people who *moved with rhythm*, they said. And they took that list and now Agatha and I both have to be in the interpret-at-at-ative dance' (she always gave it too many syllables, because once you start it's hard to stop) 'and it's going to be awful! They didn't ask if anyone wanted to be in it or not. Are we going away for Easter? Can we go to Cork, please? Or Outer Mongolia? *Anywhere?*'

'It sounds very – well – interesting, Lilac. Why don't you just wait and see what it's like before you complain about it? Anyway, you were on the altar for the concert before Christmas and you were fine. I don't see the difference, really.'

'It's *completely* different, Mum. I was part of an orchestra then, sitting down, hidden behind the flutes, mostly.'

Lilac and Agatha had actually been having a lot of fun disco dancing, but if this was the price you paid for fun, Lilac wished they hadn't. Having to dance on the steps of the altar in front of the whole parish! Probably wearing some stupid flowy gown thing – Lilac had seen interpretative dances before, and her overwhelming feeling was never one of holiness but more of mortification for the poor dancers who had to make such a show of themselves up there in public.

There was a new letter from Margery. Lilac abandoned her complaints to her mother, who obviously didn't get it at all, and opened the envelope.

Dear Lilac,

In Canada you don't make your confirmation until you're 14, in Grade 8. Mum says that's what Prodestants do at home, and she's very Put Out that they make Catholics do it too here. She asked the priest if they couldn't just do me as well, while the bishop was here anyway, but he said no. So I don't get to choose a new name at all yet. I suppose I can do it next year when we're back in Ireland. I wanted to choose Margarita, which is like Margery only much prettier. And then I could just tell people that was my name, which would be true.

Caroline and Jean-Claude aren't going out any more. I think he broke it off with her. She said her heart was broken and that she'd loved him more truely than she'd ever loved Danny in Ireland. But two days later I saw her at lunchtime definitely flirting with one of the other boys in her grade, all giggly and not like Normal Caroline. So I think she has no heart at all.

Love from
Margery

Margery's big sister Caroline was sixteen and seemed to have a lot of Boy Troubles. Lilac was a bit confused about Jean-Claude, because that didn't even look like a boy's name to her, but apparently it was. Margery tried to explain lots about what Canada was like in her letters, but it was still very hard to imagine, and there were always things that Lilac didn't quite understand but didn't want to ask about either.

CHAPTER 5

Agatha and Lilac were walking home from school the long way, by the seafront, and Lilac was trying to explain to Agatha exactly how terrible being involved in the interpretative dance was going to be. Agatha didn't seem to be quite as glum as Lilac about it.

'That's just because you don't know so many people here, so it's not as embarrassing for you.' Agatha had only moved to their town last year. 'And you haven't ever seen an interpretative dance, so you don't know what it's really like,' Lilac told her ominously. Secretly, she was starting to think that Agatha's solo at the Christmas concert had given her a taste for the limelight and that she actually *wanted* to do the dance. Lilac was pretty sure from the way Granny sometimes spoke of people having 'a taste for the limelight' that it was a bad thing to have.

'We'll just have to deny everything. Tell people it's not us. We'll be wearing some sort of drapey thing, I'm sure – maybe there'll be a mask too, or a veil. A veil would be very church-y. Maybe we can convince Miss Taylor to give us veils, and then nobody will ever know who it is.'

But the next day Miss Taylor described her vision for the dancers to the select group she'd gathered around her just before lunchtime. They were to borrow the altar boys' spare robes, which were long and white, and they'd put bright red sashes on them to denote the joy of Easter. There would be no masks, or veils, or anything to hide behind, and long hair was to be tied back so it wouldn't obscure 'your beautiful godly faces' as Miss Taylor so happily put it. They were to meet in the hall after school the next day to start learning their movements. 'It won't be difficult, ladies, it'll be fun. The overall effect should be dramatic and also spiritually uplifting for the congregation.'

Miss Taylor always called them ladies, never girls. In Lilac's opinion, she was the sort of junior infants' teacher who was just a few degrees away from being a nun. She had short brown hair and was old but not very old, maybe around forty. She never wore any makeup, not even a little pink lipstick, and she liked tweedy skirts and brown lace-up shoes. She was particularly musical, so she often worked with the older children on things like this, and of course she'd known each of them since they'd been four, which she always liked to bring up in conversation.

'Ah, Adele Duffy, I remember you sucking your thumb in my classroom on your first day of school, you wouldn't say boo to a goose. And now look at you, all get-up-and-go.' Adele would happily have got up and gone right then, rather than suffer this trip down memory lane. She tossed her hair and chewed imaginary gum, trying to look cool. Lilac didn't dare giggle in case she drew attention to herself. She didn't remember much about junior infants, but no doubt Miss Taylor would have some story for her too, and she wasn't eager to hear it. Agatha, having only come to the school last September, didn't have the same problem, but her little brother was in Miss Taylor's class this year, and Miss Taylor always seemed to have a message for her to pass on or something she should persuade him to do.

'Agatha, now, tell your mother that Peter is a dote, so he is, but he's a contrary one too. Maybe you can convince him not to pour his free milk on his sandwiches again, can you do that? I'm sure he'll listen to you. The government doesn't give it to us so that he can waste it, I told him today.' Agatha was certain that pint-sized Peter would quite happily ruin his sandwiches every day of the year if he ever heard that people specifically wanted him not to. 'I'll try,' she mumbled, resolving never to say a word about it.

'Now off you go and eat your lunches, ladies, and I'll see you after school tomorrow. Don't forget!' Miss Taylor was exactly as cheery as anyone who voluntarily spent all day with a room full of four year olds had to be. Lilac sat beside Agatha in the yard, eating a marmalade sandwich and feeling as if all the energy had been drained out of her just by trying to defend herself against the cheerfulness.

'It's going to be awful,' she said. Agatha just nodded and morosely bit into her apple. She was convinced.

CHAPTER 6

Lilac's dad was making a sandwich, carefully pressing a single leaf of lettuce on top of delicate slices of cheese and tomatoes, exactly sized to the slice of bread underneath. Gerry liked to think of his sandwiches as miniature works of art.

'Want a sandwich, Lilac?' he asked, standing back a little to consider his creation from various angles. 'Mum's gone into town with her cronies; it's just you and me this evening.'

'Not really. I have to give Guzzler a snuggle,' Lilac said. First things first. She went to commune with the dog for a few minutes. Then her tummy rumbled and she decided she did want a sandwich after all so she went back into the kitchen. Gerry was sitting at the table with the *RTÉ Guide* propped up in front of his plate, reading an article about *Glenroe*. 'I thought you hated *Glenroe*,' Lilac said, as she got out the marmalade. She didn't like cheese sandwiches very much. They were too cheesy.

'I do. Agricultural proletarian nonsense. I'm reading this

to see why anyone would watch it.'

'Because they want to know what happens. Just like Mum does. And you do too, or you wouldn't come and watch it on Sunday nights.'

'I just don't want to miss the news, that's why I'm there.'

Lilac gave him her best sceptical look, and he stuck his tongue out at her. Then she suddenly remembered something.

'Dad! I found a silver box on the beach but it's stuck shut. Can you open it?'

'You did? Hmm. Well, I don't know. You'll have to show it to me. How big is it? Does it have pirates' booty in it? Pieces of eight?'

'Maybe, but I don't think so. It's small. I'll get it.' She ran upstairs and had to think for a minute before she remembered where she'd hidden it, behind her swimming togs at the back of her third drawer. There it was, still shiny. She took it back downstairs.

'See?' She demonstrated how the lid didn't open by vigorously failing to open it.

'I see, I see,' he said, taking it from her. 'Well, I'll see what I can do. Not right now, Lilac, sit down and eat your dinner. Is that all you're having? A marmalade sandwich? Will that do you?'

'If I'm hungry later I'll have some cereal.' Actually, Lilac was sort of hoping she'd be hungry later, because there were still the Coco Pops from the variety pack to be dealt with. And somehow, cereal always tasted even more delicious at any time of day that wasn't breakfast. '*Please* will you see if you can open it straight after you eat your food?' A sandwich, no matter how artistically constructed, did not seem to deserve the word dinner.

'After I've had my cuppa. A man's cuppa is sacrosanct, not to be dismissed lightly.'

'Sigh,' said Lilac as sarcastically as she could.

Her dad didn't spend too long over his cup of tea after all. Usually he loved nothing better than to frustrate Lilac when she was impatient for him to do something, but he was curious about the box too. They took it down the garden to his shed, with Guzzler following interestedly behind them. Guzzler had found the box, after all, Lilac supposed. He had a right to know what was in it. Though if it was anything other than puppy treats, he probably wouldn't care.

In the shed, Gerry took some time selecting a small hammer. He stood poised with it an inch above the crumpled corner of the box, considering how best to approach it. Then he put the hammer back down and picked up a pliers, which he applied gently to one shiny side, but there was nothing to get a grip on. He picked the hammer back up for a moment and put it down again. Next he tried to wedge a small flat-headed screwdriver under the lid, hoping to lever it up, but it wouldn't even fit in between the two layers of metal.

'This isn't as easy as it looks, Lilac,' he said. She could see that, though she was itching to just pick up an implement and have a go at it herself. 'I'm afraid of damaging it even more. Maybe we should take it to someone.'

'What sort of someone, Dad?'

'Well, I don't know. I'll have to have a think about it. I might know a man. Leave it with me, now, for a few days.'

'Don't forget about it, Dad.' Gerry was not the most reliable, Lilac knew. When he was working on a painting, which he mostly was except for the times he was thinking about one but not painting it yet, he tended to have a one-track mind.

Between the picture-painting father and the novel-writing mother, Lilac thought she was lucky to ever get a birthday or Christmas present on time in her life. She always made sure to remind them early and often about such events, and usually presented them with a helpful list so they wouldn't have to wonder too much about what to get her. Of course, the list often had things like 'A griffon', 'A circus', or 'Trapeze lessons' on it, but she usually got lots of books and book tokens and coloured pencils, which she liked almost as much.

CHAPTER 7

The movements for the interpretative dance did turn out to be quite simple, as Miss Taylor had promised. But that didn't stop the girls from crashing into each other several times in each practice, because two steps in the wrong direction would inevitably take you straight into your neighbour's path. There were also hand movements that looked like a cross between sign language and the way you might try to attract attention if you were drowning in slow motion.

The hardest part was moving together, on the beat. If you waited to see what everyone else was doing, so that you definitely went the right way, you'd be too late and slow the whole dance down. And if everyone waited to see what everyone else was doing, nobody would ever start at all. Miss Taylor stood in front of them miming the movements they were supposed to be making, but at the moment it wasn't helping much.

'You need to be like synchronised swimmers, ladies. Have you ever seen synchronised swimmers?' Miss Taylor asked hopefully. Nobody had. 'Not even in the Olympics?'

'The Olympics are next year, Miss Taylor. They're called the 1988 Olympics,' someone helpfully pointed out.

'Yes, but the last ones. In 1984. Oh, I suppose you were too small to remember.'

'I remember 1984,' Agatha said. 'I was seven and I had chicken pox.'

'All year?' Lilac was aghast.

'No, but it felt like a long time. I was really itchy and I had to have baths with white stuff in them.'

'Did you do any synchronised swimming in your baths?' Adele wanted to know.

'Ladies, ladies. Back to the dance.' Miss Taylor was impatient. 'We only have a week left, you know. We should have the altar-boy robes on Monday and I'll have the material for your sashes then too. You can ask your mothers to sew them up – it will just be a simple seam. Now, places please. And one and two and . . . *Here I am, Lord, is it I, Lord* . . . ' Miss Taylor warbled the hymn's opening bars.

Agatha and Rachel Jackson crashed into each other again, and everyone had to go back to the start.

After dinner that day, Lilac opened the front door to find Michael from up the road on the front step, holding something that looked like a sheet.

'Hi.'

'Hi. I'm supposed to give you this. I don't know why, they didn't say.'

'What is it?'

31

'It's my altar-boy vestment thingy. They said your school needed all the spare ones and I still had mine at home, and then they told me to drop it in to you because you live near me. What do you need it for?'

Lilac looked down at the front step and felt a blush beginning on her cheeks. Embarrassment about blushing so easily made her blush even more. 'I can't tell you.'

'OK. Why not?'

'Because.'

'Are you going to be an altar girl? They have those in some churches.'

'Noooo. It's worse than that.'

'Ah go on, tell me.' He grinned at her.

Half of Lilac wanted to tell Michael, because he was her friend, after all, and sometimes it was fun telling someone how awful your life was. But the other half wished she had just said something casual right at the beginning of the conversation, taken the gown-thingy and closed the door. Because if he knew, he'd tell his friends, and then everyone would know and there'd be no denying it, ever. Then she had an idea.

'It's super-mega-ginormously embarrassing,' she said. 'I can only tell you if you tell me something embarrassing for you back, and then we'll both have to keep the secrets. Have you got something embarrassing you can tell me?'

Michael's whole face was suddenly tinged with pink. 'Well, actually, I sort of do have something I didn't tell you before.'

For a moment, Lilac wondered whether asking a boy to tell her a secret was a bad idea. Who knew what sort of secrets boys had? Maybe it would be something she didn't want to know at all, and she'd regret this deal to her dying day. There she'd be on her deathbed, surrounded by her children and grandchildren and news reporters and heads of state, and she'd tell them in a quavering voice, as she prepared to meet her maker, 'In all my long and dazzlingly successful life, there's just one question I wish I'd never asked . . .' But Michael was ploughing ahead with his revelation, as if it was something he really wanted to get off his chest.

'Before, when you asked me if I'd chosen my Confirmation name and I said I hadn't, that wasn't really true. It was sort of true, because I didn't get to choose it. But I know what it is. It's going to be . . .' – he took a deep breath – 'Mary.'

Lilac really didn't know what to say to that. She wrinkled her brow emphatically and waited for him to explain.

'My granny –' he went on in a rush, leaning against the side of the front door for support '– is really religious. And she made my mum promise that she'd give all of us holy names. So she did – David and Michael and James are all important in the Bible. But then Granny said we had to have even holier names for our Confirmation. And Mum says we have to do it or Granny will cut us out of her will, and she lives in this huge house in town that's worth a mint and she's never going to sell it so we have to be nice to her because Dad's business isn't going well . . . I don't think I was meant to tell you all that . . .' he trailed off, distracted for a moment.

'That's OK,' said Lilac. 'I won't say anything about it. Go on.'

'And there are the three of us to feed and clothe and put through college and all, so Mum said we just have to grin and bear it and that lots of men who were born in 1950 have Mary for a middle name because it was a Marian year whatever that means.' He finished in a hurry, bright red now.

Lilac solemnly considered Michael's tale of woe. 'That's really awful. I'm sorry.'

'So what's yours? You have to tell me now. And don't tell anyone *any* of that, not just the part about the money.'

'Of course not.' She would never divulge such a terrible secret. 'I have to wear the altar boy thing because I'm in an interpretative dance on the altar at the Family Mass on Easter Sunday.'

'Ohhh.' There was a world of understanding in that one slow syllable. Unlike Agatha, Michael knew exactly how bad that would be. 'But, hey,' he went on, more upbeat, 'this is the good bit. David's Confirmation name is even worse than Mary.'

'David your big brother? How could anything be worse than Mary-for-a-boy?'

'It's Hyacinth.'

'You're right. That's worse.'

'He would KILL me if he knew I'd told you.'

'Cross my heart and hope to die I'll never reveal it. Not under pain of death.'

Michael handed over the white gown and Lilac closed the door behind him, musing on grannies who ruled the roost and thinking to herself that at least the interpretative dance would be over in a week, but David Jennings's Confirmation name would be Hyacinth for ever.

CHAPTER 8

'Mum, you haven't asked me what sort of Easter egg I want yet', Lilac said on the Thursday of that week. 'I was thinking a Mars Bar one, because they come with a whole king-sized Mars Bar, and there's probably something else inside the egg too. But maybe a Flake one because I really like Flakes. Yes, I think a Flake one, actually. Unless you've already got me a surprise one.' Lilac could be extra thoughtful sometimes.

'Easter? No, Easter's not *this* weekend. It can't be.'

'I'm on Easter holidays.' Lilac started to count off the days on her fingers. 'Yesterday was Spy Wednesday. Today is Holy Thursday. Tomorrow is Good Friday. Saturday doesn't have a name. And Sunday is Easter Sunday, when my life as a not-yet-mortified member of our parish will end. Remember?'

'Yes. I know. I know all that, but somehow I thought there was still another week before Easter happened. Because you have a week and a half off school.'

'Yes, but Easter's in the middle, not at the end of it.'

'Of course it is. You're right. Well, no, I have to confess that we didn't already get you a surprise Easter egg. You wouldn't pop down to the supermarket and buy yourself the one you want, would you? In case they're all gone by Saturday. I suppose everything will be closed tomorrow. I'll give you the money.'

'Mum, sometimes I think you've completely given up on being a parent.'

'No, sweetheart, no. I'm just bolstering your independence, that's all. You'll thank me when you're older.'

'Maybe. But I'll still remember the time I had to buy my own Easter egg.'

Lilac took Guzzler with her and set off for the shops. On the way she passed the Jenningses' house, where Jimmy, the little one who was a holy terror, was outside digging a hole in the flowerbed with a yellow plastic spade. She couldn't see his face, just his white-blonde hair bobbing up and down as he worked away, engrossed. 'Hi, Jimmy,' Lilac said as she passed. 'What are you up to?'

'Not nothin',' said Jimmy, which was his standard response when he was doing something he shouldn't be. Lilac decided not to investigate further. She pulled Guzzler away from the interesting smells he'd found at the gatepost and went on her way.

At the supermarket, the selection was not great. The Mars Bar eggs were all gone and the pyramid-shaped display looked as if it had had a bite taken out of it by a chocolate-and-foil-loving giant. Or maybe, Lilac thought, a giant whose digestive system could filter out the cardboard boxes and shiny foil around the eggs and just get to the chocolate. Then again, giants probably needed lots of fibre. Maybe cardboard was good for them. It would certainly be filling.

Triumphantly, Lilac located a lone Flake egg at the back of the display and ran to the cash register with it, before anyone else could grab it out of her hands. There was some change, so she bought two Creme Eggs as an Easter present for her parents. Guzzler wasn't allowed chocolate, so he didn't get any special Easter presents, just an extra doggy treat on Sunday morning after Mass.

Lilac came out of the shop, swinging her bumpy, pointy plastic bag, to find Guzzler being talked to by a strange man. Guzzler didn't usually like strangers, but he was letting this one pet him and listening to his patter as if he was hearing all the secrets of the butcher's back room where the biggest bones were kept.

'Hello,' Lilac said in a not-very-friendly voice, as she untwisted Guzzler's lead from the railing. 'He's my dog.' That was probably obvious, but she felt as though she had to say something.

The man looked up with a big smile, immune to her coolness. 'He's a great fellow, so he is. What's his name? He has some boxer in there, does he, and a bit of collie too?' The man was younger than Lilac's dad, but he wore the sort of tweed cap that old men wear. It looked strange on him, but maybe it was a fashion statement.

'We don't know; we got him from the animal rescue people when he was a puppy. His name's Guzzler.' Because he eats people, she wanted to add. She didn't like this friendly man and his familiar ways with her dog. 'We have to go now.'

The man gave Guzzler one last head rub and said, 'Bye, Guzzler, nice to meet you. And you too.' He nodded at Lilac and went on up the hill.

Lilac should have gone back up the hill too, to get home, but she didn't want to follow straight after the man, so she went down the street and turned right, planning to walk three sides of a square and arrive home from the opposite direction instead.

'Who was he, Guzzler?' she asked as they went. 'Why was he being nice to you? Why were you listening to him? Did he smell of cats?' Guzzler didn't answer, though at the word 'cats' he pricked up his ears and looked around hopefully. 'No cats, boy. Let's just go home,' Lilac said, 'before it rains on us.'

The first big drops of rain were falling as they turned onto the far end of Lilac's road. They came plopping down in fat, cold drops between the mostly bare tree branches, where the buds were just starting to send out bright green leaves. Lilac broke into a run, with Guzzler happy to gallop in front of her, straining at his lead. They reached the front door in a mad dash, only a little damp, just before the heavens opened. Lilac stood in the shelter of the little portico over the door, panting, and watched people here and there scurrying to stay dry – all except for one man, on the other side of the road, who wore a tweed cap and didn't change his stride one bit, as the rain came down in a sheet, to soak into the ground and make the daffodils grow taller.

CHAPTER 9

On Saturday night Lilac ran downstairs waving the piece of red material that was supposed to be a sash by the following morning. 'Mum! Mum! You have to sew this! I nearly forgot!'

Lilac's mother looked up serenely from the newspaper crossword that kept her occupied during ad breaks in *Inspector Morse*.

'Lilac, you know I don't sew. I don't even know where I'd find a needle in the house. What is it for? Surely you don't need it right this instant.'

'I do, Mum. It's my belt-thingy for tomorrow. It goes over Michael's altar-boy dress that I have to wear.' Lilac had been doing such a great job not thinking about the interpretative dance that she hadn't even taken the red fabric out of her bag until a moment earlier. 'This is a *disaster*.'

'No, it's not.' Only an imminent writing deadline could ever ruffle her mother's composure. 'It's an opportunity to be resourceful. Now show me what you have.' She took it and turned it over in her hands. 'And you have to make it into a sash? Well, we don't need to sew for that. We can sellotape it together.'

'Mum, we can't sellotape it. It won't stick. That's a *terrible* idea.' Lilac's voice was getting a little squeaky with panic. 'Anyway, I used up all the sellotape on the collage I made last week. We could staple it if we had a stapler. Do we have a stapler?'

'No, we don't. Lilac, if you finish something off, please write it on the shopping list. You know that.'

'Sorry. Glue? Do we have any Pritt Stick? No, wait, I finished that on the collage too, before I started using the sellotape.'

'I don't think that sort of glue is meant for fabric, anyway.'

'So we're completely out of sticking things, at half past nine on Easter Saturday night? What are we going to *dooooo*?' Guzzler raised his head and gave a short howl in sympathy.

Gerry's hand paused over the sketch he'd been working on. He never relaxed in front of the telly without at least a doodle happening on his lap at the same time.

'What's this disaster, then? You need to fold it over and keep it together? Here, give it to me and I'll have it for you in the morning.'

'Dad, what will you do? Do you have glue? A needle and thread? Are you sure you can fix it in time?'

'Don't you worry, it'll be fine.'

Lilac was not convinced, but there was nothing more she could do. She went over her steps for the dance one last time in her head, and then went to bed, thinking that at least this time tomorrow it would all be over, and even if she could never be seen in public again, at least she'd have a Flake Easter egg to console herself with.

The Family Mass was at ten on Sunday mornings. Lilac was supposed to be at the church at half past nine in order to be definitely on time and ready, even though the previous Mass would only be three-quarters-way through by then and it would take no more than a minute to put their gowns on. At seven o'clock she couldn't stay in bed any longer and thumped down the stairs to the kitchen.

'Dad! Dad! Have you done it? Did you fix my sash?'

Gerry was in his morning pose: standing with tea mug in hand, head bowed beside the big old-fashioned radio, intent on hearing the headlines.

'Shush,' he said. Always an early riser, he kept the news turned down low in the mornings so as not to wake anyone else, but you interrupted it at your peril. He gestured towards the table.

Lilac looked. The place where she always sat was set with a cereal bowl and spoon, but sitting crookedly in her bowl was the Easter egg in its big square box, with the red sash tied up in a bow around it. She ran over to examine it more closely.

'Dad? What *is* this?' There appeared to be tiny nails in her interpretative-dance sash.

'Picture pins. Just like staples, practically. I hammered them in and bent them over with the pliers. It just needs a bit of a run over with the steam iron to get the creases out and it'll be grand. Mind you don't scratch the iron with the metal pins, though.'

There wasn't really time to explain to her father that this

was not quite what Miss Taylor was expecting. With a bit of luck, Miss Taylor wouldn't even spot the difference. Lilac ran for the iron and plugged it in to heat up while she ate her breakfast. 'Can I open my Easter egg? Just to see? I promise I won't eat any of it . . . unless a little bit falls off accidentally . . .' She mumbled that last part.

'All right. Just to see.'

Savouring each moment of the ritual, Lilac carefully sliced through the strip of tape that was holding the box closed. She took out the cardboard that held the top of the egg in place and slid out the clear plastic shell. This was hinged on one side, like a door, and when she opened it up the foil-wrapped chocolate egg and the Flake bar fell out onto her lap. Guzzler, roaming the kitchen in search of whatever he might find, made a dive for them, but Lilac scooped them out of his reach. 'No, Guzzler, no chocolate. Bad for you!'

She put the bar on the shelf by the biscuit tin, because she was going to save it for break time on the first day back at school after the holidays. Then she examined the egg, reverently smoothing the foil over it with a fingertip, to see if there was a pattern underneath. There seemed to be a flower etched on the front, but otherwise it was plain. She didn't rip the foil yet: it was too perfect. Then she put it back in its plastic protection and slid the whole thing back into the box. If not for the space where the bar had been, you wouldn't know it had been opened at all.

CHAPTER 10

A warm, singey smell permeated the kitchen. The iron was definitely hot enough. Lilac put a tea towel on the table and ironed the sash flat on it, going carefully around the bumps where the nails were. She could have taken out the ironing board, but that seemed like too much work for one little sash. Then she thought she should probably iron the gown while she was at it, so she ran upstairs to get that.

In her bedroom she remembered that her hair was meant to be neatly pulled back. She spent a couple of minutes vigorously brushing her curls, and then making a ponytail that was so tight it made the backs of her ears hurt. When she took her hands away most of the curls sprang back out of the bobbin into a golden halo of frizz around her face. Wishing she had smooth, shiny hair like Margery's, or even wavy but controllable hair like Agatha's, Lilac took a handful of hair clips and set about pinning all the wayward locks to the side of her head. Eventually it was done, but she looked like someone else, not herself. She took it all out again.

'Lilac! Lilac! I think something's happening with your iron, Lilac!' her father was shouting from downstairs. She dropped the brush on her bed and ran back down to a much more singey smell than before, and dark smoke curling from the iron, which was not upended as it should have been, but still face down on the red sash.

'Dad! Why didn't you take it off? It's *ruined*! I'm in *huge* trouble.' Lilac snatched up the iron and looked at the offending article in despair. There was a black triangle on the red fabric, and more on the tea towel around it.

'I only just saw it,' Gerry said. 'And it wasn't burning the house down, just smelling a little charred. Like toast.' Gerry quite liked slightly burnt toast. Extra crunchy, he would say happily, as it fell apart under his butter knife.

Lilac held up the sash for him to see. 'Look! First it has nails in it and now it's burnt. How much worse can it get?' Her voice cracked a little and tears sprang into her eyes.

'You should never say that, you know,' Gerry warned her, still unfazed. 'Tempting fate, that's what that is. Just put the burnt bit facing in. And unplug the iron next time.'

Lilac unplugged it, then trudged upstairs again blinking the tears back, her good mood ruined. Like the sash, she thought. And my hair. And everything. She sat on the bed and felt a lump rise in her throat at the injustice of the whole thing. One measly chocolate egg could not make up for all this awfulness. She was about to give in to the lump and the tears and let herself have a good big wallowing cry when her mother passed by on her way downstairs and looked cheerily into Lilac's room.

'Good morning, darling, and happy Easter! Are you all

ready for your big stage debut?'

'No. It's all terrible. It's not a stage debut, it's an altar debut. And I want to run away.'

Her mother sat on the bed beside her. 'If you run away, you can't take your Easter egg with you. I'll keep it as tax. Anyway, you'd need to travel light.'

This was an obvious ploy to humour her. Lilac wasn't going along with it. She fell backwards on her duvet and rolled over to hide her face. She still hadn't quite decided whether or not to let out the dramatic wail that was building up inside her.

'They'll need someone to fill in for you in the dance. Maybe I could do it. Or Dad. He's quite the twinkletoes, you know, when the mood takes him. I'm sure he'd do it for Jesus.'

The idea of Gerry on the altar with five ten-year-old girls, trying to keep up with an interpretative dance he'd never learned, was too much for Lilac, even though it was patently ridiculous. She snorted into her pillow.

'I'll go down and ask him,' her mother said, as she rose from the bed and smoothed her skirt.

Lilac spent five minutes having something between a laughing fit and a sobbing jag into her pillow, then sat up and looked in the mirror. 'You can't go around it,' she told herself. 'You just have to go through it.' She squared her shoulders like a soldier going over the top, she decided, and swallowed hard. The lump was still in her throat, but it wasn't so big any more. She got dressed quickly in jeans and her lucky palest-pink jumper (no need for a fancy Easter dress, at least, since she'd be covered up by the altar-boy vestment), took the white gown and her hairbrush and clips, and went downstairs to find her parents doing a foxtrot around the kitchen to a Frank Sinatra number on the radio.

'Dancing's in the McCarthy blood,' her father announced as they ended with a twirly flourish. 'Do you think Michael's altar-boy thing will fit me, or should I wear my dressing gown? It's quite respectable.' He flapped his navy, paisley-patterned dressing gown at her.

'I'm not going to dignify that with an answer,' Lilac said snootily. They couldn't make her laugh. She would be cool and collected, but she would not be amused. 'Mum, what am I going to do with my hair? It's meant to be back from my face, but when I try to make a ponytail it all comes out, and when I use clips I look like a big round sunshine with eyes.' She brandished the various hair implements at her mother.

'I can't sew a seam to save my life, and I'm certain I was meant to have a fleet of servants to cook and clean for me, but if I do say it myself I'm not bad at hair,' said Lilac's mum, as she turned Lilac around and soothingly started twisting the hair at the sides of her face around itself until she had caught all the curls and tamed them into a knot at the back of Lilac's head. She secured it with a bobbin and a few clips and sent Lilac to look in the mirror. Her face still looked like a big round sun with freckles, she thought, but it was sort of pretty too. Sophisticated, maybe. Definitely better than when she had done it herself.

'Thanks, Mum,' she said sheepishly.

Lilac plugged the iron in once more and gave the white gown a quick once over, taking out the worst of the wrinkles. 'They won't see the rest from down the church,' she said to herself. Her mother suggested they put it on a hanger instead of stuffing it into a bag to crease again, so she took a plastic hanger from the coat cupboard and hung it on that, tying the red sash loosely round the hook so it wouldn't get lost.

CHAPTER 11

At the church, Lilac went in the side door by the sacristy. It led to a little hallway where Agatha and a couple of the other girls were already waiting.

'I knew there'd be no point coming this early. There's nothing we can do while the other Mass is still on,' Adele Duffy complained. She did not have her hair neatly pulled back; it was flowing over her shoulders like a waterfall.

'I think they just wanted to make sure we'd be in good time,' said Lilac, knowing that was exactly what her mum would say but unable to stop herself. Adele's gown was also on a hanger, but hers was a puffy satin hanger, and the gown looked bright white and as if it had never seen a wrinkle in its life. The other girls were carrying plastic bags, presumably with the gowns folded up inside.

'What happened to your sash, Lilac?' Adele was looking curiously at the red bow around Lilac's hanger.

'Nothing.'

'But it has shiny things in it. And a big black splodge in the middle.'

'No it doesn't.' Lilac pulled the sash off the hanger and rolled it up into a tight spiral with the burn facing inwards.

'It's fine.'

'Uh-huh.' Adele didn't sound convinced, but she started humming 'Here I am Lord' to herself and practising her steps. She took three quick paces backwards and collided with Miss Taylor, who was just coming through the door.

'Ladies, ladies,' Miss Taylor began, because everyone was giggling furiously, 'calmness, sanctity, please. Easter is a glorious mystery indeed, but we must be serene . . . Adele, dear, did you bring something to put your hair back? I brought a few hair bobbins with me in case anyone forgot.' Miss Taylor rooted in her large handbag and produced an ugly black bobbin with two bright-red plastic balls attached. Adele wrinkled her nose. Miss Taylor delved again and brought out a hairbrush. 'Just turn around for me there, Adele, I'll see you right.' Adele had no choice but to submit, and in a surprisingly short time Miss Taylor had given her one long, tight plait straight down her back – the sort of thing that Adele would never normally wear. 'Now, don't fiddle with it, I don't want it to come loose. Anyone else?' Miss Taylor waggled a few more bobbins at them, but everyone shook their heads in terror and tried to take a step back but came up hard against the wall. In fact, they did mostly have either short hair or some sort of ponytail. Rachel Jackson's short bob had a fringe, and Agatha's wavy black hair was held back at the sides with curved, gold-coloured clips.

The first Mass must have ended, because a stream of people started to trickle out through the passageway where they were standing, and the strains of the organ recessional could be heard every time the inner door opened. Miss Taylor said, 'That's our cue, ladies!' Then she knocked on the sacristy door and opened it confidently, walking in and motioning to the girls to follow her.

A little while later the girls were all seated decorously in the front row of the side wing of the church – Ms Taylor called it the transept, but then she had to explain where she meant because nobody had heard that word before – waiting for the after-Communion time when they would do their dance. The priest's vestments were bright red, just as Miss Taylor had predicted, and the flowers all over the church and especially on the altar were spectacular. 'The flower ladies have done themselves proud today,' Miss Taylor had noted when she peeked out of the sacristy while the girls put on their gowns and tied their sashes. Lilac had to try a few times to get her sash tied the right way to hide both the black burn mark and the most obvious of the tacks, but she thought she'd managed. Agatha had checked her rear view and said it looked OK, and nobody else had noticed that Lilac's sash was not sewn but, well, more like hammered together.

The readings were long, the sermon seemed to go on for hours, the choir kept interrupting to sing things that would be much quicker to just say – like 'Alleluia', for goodness' sake, why should that take ten minutes? – and there were so many people that the queue for Communion was never-ending; but finally it was time for Lilac and her five companions to stand up and walk slowly and gracefully to their places on the low, wide steps leading up to the altar. Front and centre, in full view of the entire congregation. As they filed out, Adele put on a big cheesy grin and whispered, 'Showtime!' She waggled her hands down by her sides like a tap dancer. Lilac and Agatha tried hard not to giggle, but the nerves were getting to them and a tiny squeak escaped from somewhere between Agatha's nose and her firmly closed mouth. At this, Lilac pinched her lips together even harder, and was much too busy thinking about not snorting to remember how reverent and graceful she was meant to be.

They took their places and the sixth-class choir, up in the gallery, started to sing. 'And one and two and three . . .' Lilac heard Miss Taylor's voice in her head with the music, and luckily her feet seemed to know what they should do even though her brain was not fully intent on the job. She moved across, and back, and managed not to collide with Rachel Jackson, and up and down and . . . things were going quite well.

'OK. This is OK, I'm not thinking about the people watching. I'm just concentrating on the steps,' she thought to herself. And with that, she thought about the people watching, took a step to the left instead of the right, and bumped into a huge vase of flowers that definitely hadn't been there when they'd rehearsed last week.

As if in slow motion, Lilac put her hand out but couldn't stop the vase from toppling over with a thud. The flowers splayed onto the ground, but they were stuck in green foam stuffed into the neck of the container, so they couldn't go far. She hesitated for a moment wondering if she should try to pick up the giant urn, then decided not to and scrambled back to roughly where she should have been. She tried to go on as if nothing had happened, but she was two steps behind everyone else and the giggle she'd been stifling earlier seemed to want to come out again. She caught Adele's eye and thought 'Showtime!' and suddenly her whole body was shaking with silent laughter.

The music was slowing down and the dance was coming to an end – the six dancers had to meet in the middle of the altar facing one another with their arms stretched out and slightly back over their heads – 'like a flower', Miss Taylor had said. Miss Taylor had thought it would be easier for them to face inwards than outwards, staring at the congregation, as they held the pose; but she hadn't reckoned with a fit of the giggles. Agatha closed her eyes so she didn't have to see the others, but that just made it worse. By the time they had counted five very slow beats and could take their arms down, all six girls were convulsed with laughter and very red in the face from trying not to make a sound. They returned to their seats certain that they were in huge disgrace, especially Lilac, but Miss Taylor just smiled serenely and whispered, 'Very nice, ladies.'

Michael came over to Lilac outside the church, while the adults were all saying Happy Easter to each other and talking about the weather and whether it would rain for the bank holiday tomorrow. 'Your dance wasn't that bad,' he said encouragingly. 'Though I held my breath when you knocked the flowers over. I thought water would spill everywhere but it didn't, so that was good.'

Lilac nodded. 'I know. I thought we'd have to finish the dance in a big puddle. My dad's already made a joke about Swan Lake. *Lake.*' She sighed dramatically.

'What were the shiny things in your belt? They sparkled every time you passed through the beam of sunlight. It looked cool. But none of the others had them.'

'Um. Yeah. No, nobody else did.' Lilac wasn't sure what to say about that. 'It was awful, we were all *dying* laughing. I will never ever be so mortified in front of the whole church again as long as I live . . . Anyway, you can have your dress back.' She handed him the hanger with the white gown safely back on it. The sash was rolled up in her pocket, where nobody could comment on its appearance.

'It's not a dress,' he said, offended. But he had to take it, and as soon as she handed it over Lilac felt light and airy, as if all her worries had just floated away. A chocolate egg sat waiting for her at home, it would be her birthday in two weeks, and Easter was really a pretty good time of year after all.

CHAPTER 12

Dear Margery,

Happy Easter!

The dance is over and that's all I'm going to say about that. We had the new priest for the Mass and his sermon was very very long. I almost wanted Father Byrne back because at least he was quick. I don't think he ever put much thought into his sermons since he was so busy planning his big heist, but this new fellow seems to have nothing else to do. At least, that's what Dad says.

Important chocolate news: I got a Flake egg from my parents (though I had to go and buy it myself because my parents are completely hopeless) and then the next day we went to my aunty's and I got a Smarties egg. I have a lot of chocolate now.

Oh, some exciting gossip! Maura Rooney's house was burgled. She decided to dust for fingerprints so that she could find the culprit and bring him (or her) to justice. She ruined the carpet and her mother's good blusher brush with flour and couldn't find any fingerprints. Then it turned out that they hadn't been burgled after all, her aunty had just called round and borrowed some stuff. Her mum is really angry but I'm not sure if it's with the aunty or with Maura.

I heard Mum say that there really were some burgurlaries at the houses of people at the tennis club, but maybe Maura's aunty just called round to them too. Maura wants to be like Nancy Drew but I think she's got a long way to go.

Love from Lilac

Dear Lilac,

The idea of Maura being Nancy Drew is very funny. She'd have to keep her socks pulled up, for one thing, and she's much too cool for that.

I did not get one single egg and it's not fair. They don't do proper Easter eggs here. They have little plastic ones with about one penny sweet in them and they have egg hunts for little kids except they just put the eggs out on the grass so it's really an egg grab, not a hunt.

We went to the mall (that's the shopping centre) and

everyone was queuing up to get their kids' photos taken with the Easter Bunny and Caroline said really loudly right there beside the queue 'That's the most terrifyingly evil giant bunny costume I've ever seen' and the man with the camera gave Caroline a LOOK and I think we can never go back there again. But she was right. Half the children were crying already. After Caroline said that the other half started.

I don't think Caroline is going to be any good at her new babysitting job, but she says she needs to earn enough money to fly to Ireland at the start of the summer instead of the end. Now that it's all over with Jean-Claude she wants to get back together with Danny at home instead, but he's going to college in Galway next year so she has to get there before the summer's over to convince him that it's True Love and then they'll have a Long Distance Relationship and see each other at the weekends when he comes home for his mum to do his laundry.

I think it must be very tiring to be Caroline. It's exhausting just being her sister.

Luv,

Margery

Lilac thought so too.

Michael looked out the gate as Lilac and Guzzler went past his house the next day. He was meant to be weeding the driveway, so he needed distraction.

'I thought your granny was meant to be visiting for Easter. Did she not come?'

'Not for Easter itself,' Lilac said. 'She's coming next weekend because it's my birthday as well as Confirmation.'

'Where does she live again?'

'In Cobh, near Cork. She moved there because she's a secret agent. At least, I think she is, because she won't ever tell us why she moved. She says it was for the regatta, but she doesn't really know one end of a boat from the other.'

'The bow is the pointy end. Everyone knows that.'

Lilac made a face at him. 'I was speaking *metaphorically*. Anyway, I don't think Granny does.'

'If she's a secret agent, maybe she can solve our mystery. I think we were burgled. David and me are missing stuff and Dad can't find a silver heirloom he says was in his desk.'

'What sort of heirloom? What is an heirloom?'

'I don't know, something your grandad left you, I think.'

'Is it for weaving? Weaving air? How do you weave air?'

'Not that sort of loom. This one's just a thing he keeps stuff in. And my walkman's headphones have disappeared and David can't find a present he says he bought for his girlfriend.'

'David has a girlfriend?' It was Lilac's turn to be distracted from the topic at hand. David always seemed droopy and uninteresting. She couldn't imagine him with a girlfriend.

'I'm not sure. He might be just trying to impress us. But

he said he bought her earrings and now he can't find them. And it's not like Jimmy or I want earrings, so for once he's not accusing us of stealing them.'

'Probably it's like Maura Rooney's house and someone borrowed them. Did your aunty come round?'

'No.' Michael was adamant. 'I don't know who Maura Rooney is but no, they're really missing.'

Lilac remembered something. 'Hey, you really might have been burgled. Some people at my mum's tennis club had stuff stolen from their houses. Will I get Granny on the case? Or I could bring Guzzler over and maybe he could sniff where they were and follow the trail to the robbers' hideout and we could get everything back. And then the mayor would give us the keys to the city.'

'Yeah, right.' He pondered for a moment. 'I'd prefer a big reward. The city doesn't even have a gate to lock.'

Mrs Jennings looked out the open front door. 'Michael! You're meant to be weeding! I'm not paying you twenty pence to talk to Lilac all day.'

'I'd better get back to it,' Michael said, indicating the proliferation of tiny green shoots poking through the driveway's gravel.

Lilac said bye, pulled Guzzler away from the gatepost's smells, as always, and wondered if her mum would pay her to weed their driveway. But she quite liked the soft cushions of moss that popped up at the seams of the concrete surface, so she decided not to offer.

Agatha and her family had gone on a very special trip to Hungary, where she had uncles and aunts and a granny, for the second half of the Easter holidays, so Lilac had nobody to call for when she went for a walk up the hill a few days later. Michael was out, and he wasn't a going-for-walks-with friend anyway. She felt like she was nearly good enough friends with Jenny O'Herlihy to be on 'calling for' terms, but not quite. Maybe after her birthday party, because Jenny would be coming to that.

Since Lilac's birthday weekend was also the Confirmation weekend, when her classmates would be celebrating with their families, Lilac's party was going to be the week afterwards. Lilac had put a lot of careful thought into her invitation list. Then her mum had met someone new to the town at the tennis club and insisted on asking her eleven-year-old daughter along too.

'But, Mum,' Lilac had said, 'she won't know any of us.'

'Exactly. This is an opportunity for her to make some new friends. It's hard when you move somewhere new. You need people to make an effort.'

'But she goes to a different school. Those people will make an effort. Why does she need other friends from my school?'

'Lilac, that's enough. She's coming to your party. It will be fine.'

Her mother seemed to think they were all still five years old and would just play on the swings and in the sandpit with any other child who happened along. It wasn't like that any more, she thought – though it would be nice if it was. You had to be the right sort of person for the other people. What if this girl was very fashionable, or very snooty, or thought Lilac and her friends were all weird and not cool? Because Lilac knew that she herself was not,

59

particularly, cool. She knew Agatha was even less cool, and Margery was somewhat cool – but Margery didn't count because she wouldn't be at the party. Jenny O and Katie Byrne were also invited, and Lilac would have liked to ask Michael except of course she couldn't because he'd be the only boy. And now this girl – Evelyn was her name – and Lilac had no idea what she would be like. She'd tried to ask her mum, but it hadn't worked.

'She's a girl, Lilac, like you. Her mother's very nice and she has a marvellous backhand. A steady follow through, that's the trick to it.'

That was no help whatsoever. She would just have to wait and see.

So now Lilac took Guzzler and walked up the hill. It was a sometimes-sunny breezy April day that was almost warm enough go without a jacket (but not quite). As she got closer to the top of the hill she was very glad of her windcheater, because the gentle breeze was more like a gale blowing right across the point of land from one side to the other, with only a few gorse bushes to block its path. Lilac stayed well back from the side of the path where Agatha had nearly fallen last Christmas, even though it was now very sturdily protected by a new, stronger fence. Guzzler always veered inland just there too, nudging her to one side protectively. 'You're such a good boy, Guzzler,' Lilac said to him, remembering the dramatic rescue scene.

They didn't spend long at the top because the wind was too cold, though the sea was fun to look at, with patches of blue and greenish grey moving like a constantly shifting bedspread as the clouds briskly crossed the sun and then moved on. There were white horses on the little choppy waves and a big ship on the horizon aiming for Dublin port. The point where the sea met the sky was sharp and clear, dark blue against palest grey.

She turned her back on the expanse of windy water and headed on down the other side, to curve around the big looping trail. A little way along, there was a small gazebo set back from the footpath, where Lilac often liked to sit and pretend she was a lady of the olden days. She headed for it, letting Guzzler off the lead to root around a bit nearby. There was nobody in sight and she knew he wouldn't run off. He wasn't a running-off sort of dog.

Lilac had stepped into the gazebo and registered the instant peace of being out of the wind before she noticed that it was already occupied. There were two people there, in fact, close together on the little seating ledge around the inside. She couldn't see their faces: 'canoodling' was the word that came instantly to her mind. One of them looked up, startled, at exactly the same moment that Lilac began to turn around and duck back out as quickly as she could. As she ran back to pick up Guzzler's lead and get out of sight as soon as possible, her brain belatedly released the information it had just taken in: the face she had seen belonged to Jeannie McGrath, her babysitter.

CHAPTER 13

'There's nothing wrong with Jeannie kissing a boy,' Lilac told herself as she walked briskly down the hill pretending hard that nothing had happened, Guzzler galumphing along behind her. 'She's sixteen. Teenagers have boyfriends. It's perfectly normal.' She was mortally embarrassed that she had walked in on them, and that Jeannie had been the one to see her – if the boy had been the one who looked up, he wouldn't have known her; and she'd never have known it was Jeannie kissing him, for that matter.

Yet she felt, somehow, that Jeannie had betrayed her. Jeannie had said she didn't have a boyfriend. Of course, that was months ago and things change – you had only to think about Margery's sister Caroline, who went through boyfriends like bars of chocolate, to know that – but still. Now Jeannie was on the other side. She isn't 'just like me, only older' any more, Lilac thought. She's one of *them*.

As Lilac passed the playground at the end of her road, she saw Jimmy Jennings with his plastic shovel again. It seemed odd that there was nobody else around.

'Are you on your own?' she asked him.

'My mum knows I'm here,' he said, covering something over quickly with sand.

'Oh, OK. Well, I think it's starting to rain so maybe you should go home soon.'

'No thanks.'

She felt she'd done her duty as his elder. If he didn't want to go home till he was wet, that was his problem.

At home, Lilac started a new letter to Margery to tell her the very important gossip that Jeannie the babysitter had a boyfriend. Or at least, was kissing someone. Margery didn't know Jeannie, but she'd heard all about her in letters, since she'd started babysitting Lilac last autumn. Lilac's blue pen ran out of ink and she was scrabbling around for another in the kitchen drawer-of-all-things when the doorbell rang.

Her mother was upstairs working, so Lilac went to answer it. She couldn't reach the spyhole she was meant to peep out of first, and it was probably just Michael or the parish priest or someone anyway, so she opened it without checking. An oldish man stood there in a pair of paint-stained jeans and a zipped-up tracksuit top. His face had a lot of wrinkles and his hair was very short and silvery. He didn't exactly smile at her, but he spoke as if they knew each other.

'Ah, there you are now. Would you be a grand girl and let me take a quick look out your upstairs back window? I'm going to be doing some work on the house next door and I need to get a good look at their roof, you know yourself how it is.'

Lilac didn't know herself how it was at all, not being an

expert on roofs. But she was fairly sure she shouldn't just let this man into the house without checking first. Guzzler wandered up the hallway from his bed in the kitchen and a low growl came from his throat. It was so low that Lilac barely heard it. She was sure the man couldn't have, but just the sight of Guzzler seemed to put him off a bit. His air of certainty faltered, and though he'd looked for a moment as if he was just going to walk right in without waiting for her answer, he stepped back a little instead.

'I can't let you in right now. Come back later maybe,' Lilac said, and closed the door before the man could even answer. She knew that was rude, but it was a bit strange that he hadn't even asked if her parents were at home. Everyone else at the door or on the phone always did. But her mum must have been so engrossed in her writing that she hadn't heard the bell, because she hadn't even shouted down the stairs to find out who it was.

Lilac went back to the important job of finding a blue pen, because her writing would get messy if she had to change to black in the middle of a page.

Jeannie's meant to be coming over on Friday night because Mum and Dad and Granny are going to the tennis club musical. It's going to be really awkward. (Seeing Jeannie, I mean, not the musical. Though I'd say that'll be pretty bad too. Dad groans every time Mum mentions it, but he has to go because she's in it.) Anyway. Should I pretend it never happened or do you think she'll tell me all about it? Maybe she's in love and she wants to talk about him all the time. She'd hardly be kissing someone she wasn't in love with. Not in the gazebo on top of the hill in the middle of the afternoon. I think. Unless it's hormones. Mum told me hormones make young people do terrible things. I think they're like germs. I hope I don't catch them ever.

She left the letter there because her dad had come home and it was almost time to go and collect Granny from the train station in Dublin. She changed into one of Granny's jumpers, since she wouldn't see anyone she knew at the train station. Ever since Granny had got herself a knitting machine, the number of woolly jumpers received by Lilac and all her cousins had increased dramatically, and Lilac now had a range to choose from. Since they were sometimes not exactly to her taste, she always tried to wear them when Granny would see her but nobody else might. She selected the bright green angora one with the red triangle design this time. It made her feel like a furry Christmas tree in April.

Gerry and Lilac drove up to Heuston Station, where the Cork train came in. The traffic was all going in the other direction for rush hour, so it didn't take too long. Lilac was allowed to sit in the front seat, since she was almost eleven. Everything felt closer from there, and it was a bit scary as her dad swerved around city corners, making loud comments as if the other drivers could hear him (except then he would have been more polite). She hung on to the door handle with one hand and surreptitiously checked that her seatbelt was definitely clicked in with the other.

'Blast! Now I'm in the wrong lane!' said Gerry, flicking on his indicator and winding down his window to fling out an arm as well, so that the traffic behind him would see that he was really serious about wanting to turn here. Lilac sat up extra straight and tried to look as friendly as she could, and when the car behind and one over kindly left a gap for them to move to the next lane, she turned around and gave them a grateful smile and a polite wave so they'd know she and her dad were good people who hadn't done it on purpose. The driver waved back at her, which was nice. At least, she thought it was a wave.

Gerry finally parked a bit of a way down the quay instead of looking for a spot in the car park, because he said it would be full. He always said that. Lilac was pretty sure he'd never parked in the car park belonging to the place he was actually going to in his life.

They were a bit late, so Lilac ran ahead. The Cork train had already arrived, but Granny was sitting calmly on a bench chatting about fly fishing with an old man in a tweed cap. She didn't know the first thing about fly fishing, but Granny could talk to anyone about anything. As soon as she saw Lilac, she began to gather her various coats and bags and brightly coloured scarves, still talking and nodding away to her new friend – only to put them all back down again straight away to give Lilac a big hug and a kiss. Gerry straggled in and got a hug too, and then he picked up the biggest bag and put another over his shoulder. Lilac took two smaller ones and that left Granny with just her three coats to carry as she said goodbye and wished the man in the cap the best of luck with his catch.

'I didn't know what the weather would be doing, or

exactly what this Swiss Cottage place would be like that we're going to for the big dinner, so I thought I should just bring them all,' she explained with a wink as they walked back out to head for the car. Granny had many talents, but packing light was not one of them. She had swirled all the scarves around her neck and one was flapping behind her in the wind like a bright red pennant. It made Lilac think of the boats she'd seen at the regatta when they'd visited Granny last year.

'How did you get all this to the station in Cork?' Lilac aksed. 'And it's the Swiss Chalet, not the Swiss Cottage. I'm not sure how posh it is either because I haven't been there before, but my friend Jenny has. And practically everyone else in the class. It's the coolest place now.'

'Oh, well, in that case maybe I should have brought my fluorescent green socks but I think I forgot them. They're all the rage these days, aren't they? And I must say that's a lovely jumper you're wearing.' Granny grinned at Lilac and for a moment Lilac wasn't entirely sure how much of that was a joke. It would be awful, she thought, if Granny kept giving me these terrible jumpers just to see if I'd wear them even though she knew they were horrible. No, she decided. Granny would never do that.

'I brought you a new one too, a little birthday present. I hope you like it,' Granny went on. 'But it's a surprise, so not another word now on the subject until the big day.'

At least Lilac had a new outfit already bought for her Confirmation so there'd be no possibility of wearing Granny's jumper, whatever it might look like, to dinner that day.

CHAPTER 14

Granny was Lilac's mum's mum. Lilac's grandparents on her dad's side had both died before Lilac was born. Granny's husband, Grandad Martin, had died when Lilac was six, because he was ten years older than Granny and he'd had a heart attack. Granny was in her seventies now, which was not so old, and she was very spry and sprightly. That was how Gerry always described her when he was talking to Nuala about her mother. 'Your mother is perfectly spry and sprightly and doesn't need me to go and mow her lawn or fix her roof,' he'd say whenever Nuala suggested a trip to Cork to see if her mother was OK. 'She has a phalanx of young men down there to do her bidding, all those strapping sons of her next-door neighbours. You know they'll look after her.'

'But she's not their family. They shouldn't feel they have to. And I don't want her to feel abandoned by us.' Nuala would answer.

'*By us?* We're the ones who should feel abandoned, if anyone should!' Gerry was still a little upset that Granny had moved to Cork and taken her free babysitting service with her, not to mention the excellent Sunday dinners she used to dish up when she lived in Dublin. Lilac missed her too, but Granny came to see them often, as well as travelling to exciting faraway places. She didn't really have room for visitors in her tiny cottage by the harbour, but she said when Lilac was a bit older she could go down on the train any time and sleep on the sofa.

It took longer to get home than it had to drive up, but Granny wanted to know all about Lilac's Confirmation preparations and about Easter (she had an egg for Lilac too, she said) and the birthday plans, and which of Lilac's friends she would meet and who her teacher was and all the things Lilac wanted to tell her. It was very easy to talk to Granny; she always asked the right questions and didn't interrupt to tell you what she thought you should do. Lilac talked happily most of the way home and only remembered to ask Granny how she was when they were turning onto their road.

'Oh, I'm fine, thank you for asking. My hip's a bit sticky and I have a bruise where Daniel O'Dwyer hit me with a shuttlecock at badminton last night, the young bowsie, but I'm quite all right.' Granny coached badminton at the pensioners' club in her spare time. Daniel O'Dwyer was probably about sixty, Lilac was sure. Granny never ever seemed like an old person to Lilac. She was just herself, one of a kind: never changing, but nearly always surprising.

By the time they had dinner, Lilac had finally told Granny everything she could think of, and she was content to sit while the grown-ups chatted, picking the edible bits –

meat, carrots, potato, *maybe* celery – out of her stew and leaving the pieces of onion and parsnip behind. She was having a conversation in her head between the potato and the parsnip, which looked so similar when cut into chunks and put in a stew, but tasted so very different, so she wasn't really paying attention to what they were saying, until something about a burglary caught her ear.

'. . . been a few lately. TVs and videos and silver and jewellery too. It seems they get in around the back of the houses where people are less careful about locking up properly . . .' Lilac's mum was saying.

Lilac didn't look up, but she started to listen more carefully. When adults thought you weren't interested in the conversation, they included more of the juicy details.

'Terrible!' Granny sounded politely shocked. 'But you're always very careful about locking up, aren't you?'

'Yes, yes. Anyway, I've nothing much worth stealing when it comes to jewellery or silver.' Lilac's mother sounded a little rueful.

'And we've no video machine, so they'd be wasting their time in this house. A drop more, Angela?' Lilac's dad tilted the bottle of wine in Granny's direction.

'Not at all, thank you, Gerard. Anyway, Guzzler would chase anyone away, wouldn't he? He'd bark the house down if someone came round the back at night.' Granny sounded reassuring, as if maybe she realised Lilac was not quite as engrossed in making an onion-bits mountain in her lake of gravy as she was pretending to be.

'He would, of course. Of course!' said Lilac's mum, standing up and beginning to clear the plates. 'Now, who's for apple crumble? Custard or ice-cream? Lilac, you can stop pretending you're going to eat any more of that. Go and look in the freezer for me and see if there's any vanilla.'

Lilac had been just about to ask Granny about helping to find Michael's missing things, but five minutes of rooting through the big freezer to see if any of the tubs of Strawberry Blonde and Raspberry Ripple and Neapolitan were actually just plain Vanilla sent it right out of her head.

After apple crumble, the grown-ups had coffee and Lilac broke into Granny's Easter egg, which was actually an almost life-sized chocolate bunny. She ate the ears first, and then made the bunny hop around saying 'I'm sorry, I didn't quite hear that, what did you say?' until her parents told her it had been funny the first three times but now it was getting annoying. Granny didn't say anything, because she was always a good audience. Then they all played a game of Scrabble, which Granny won by putting 'azure' on a triple word score.

When bedtime came, Lilac was busy telling Granny her plans for the doll's house renovation she was hoping her dad would help with. She needed him to donate paint and maybe also some wood, and carpentry tuition. If she could get Granny on her side, she thought, it would be much easier to persuade Dad that she really did need her own hammer and saw so that she could make it herself once he showed her how. Granny was enthusiastic, as she always was about plans, no matter what they were.

'See, Dad, Granny thinks I should do it,' was Lilac's parting shot as she headed for bed. Guzzler raised his head lazily from his doggy bed in the corner of the room and whined a little 'night-night' whine at her, and she felt safe knowing he was there.

CHAPTER 15

Friday night arrived and Jeannie was coming to babysit. Granny was all ready to go, wearing pearls and bright lipstick and an orange-and-yellow scarf that seemed to be about six feet long; it practically trailed on the ground while still wrapping several times around her neck. Lilac loved to stroke it, because it was made of silk so soft that her fingers almost couldn't even feel it. She put it up against her cheek and moved it back and forth. Granny smelled of rose petals and hand cream, and she had the loveliest things.

'Can I have this scarf when you die, Granny?' Lilac said.

'Of course you can.' Granny never minded being asked things like that, though Lilac wouldn't have said it if her mum had been within earshot. She didn't like talk of people dying.

Lilac's mum flitted about collecting all the things she couldn't possibly forget. It was odd to see her not dressed up to go out when everyone else was, but just looking normal in her everyday clothes, because of course she was in the production. The tennis club put on a musical every year, which mostly involved people singing the songs while dressed representatively as a chorus, but this year they were branching out and having some actual scenes and major characters and solos too. Nuala was playing the lead role, for which she wore tan slacks and a cream blouse knotted at the front, with a red checked tea towel to wrap her hair up in. She would be singing 'I'm going to wash that man right out of my hair'. Gerry said he was braced for lots of *hilarious* comments from the other husbands.

At half past seven on the dot, the doorbell rang and Lilac let Jeannie in. With her mum busy in a tizzy and Granny to be introduced, there was no time to be awkward about the last time they'd seen each other, so Jeannie just came in and left her anorak on the bannisters the way she always did. Lilac put it where it was supposed to go, and followed her into the sitting room, where Granny was already asking Jeannie about school and how her mother was and all the polite but not nosy questions Granny always knew how to ask to put a stranger at ease. Jeannie even smiled as she answered, which was not something Lilac had ever seen before when Jeannie was talking to a grown-up.

Lilac's mum finally chivvied everyone out the front door and Lilac and Jeannie were left alone. Lilac dashed to turn on the television before the silence became too obvious, because she really didn't know what to say. 'Was that your boyfriend?' seemed rude, as if Lilac thought Jeannie would kiss a boy who wasn't her boyfriend – or as if he might in fact be someone else's boyfriend. 'What does it feel like when you kiss someone?' was out of the question. 'Did he kiss you first or did you kiss him first? How did you know what to do? How is it not gross?' These were all things she and Margery had wondered about together (because Caroline was not the chatty sort of big sister), but now that a normally friendly teenager with all the answers was right here in Lilac's sitting room, the notion of plunging into that conversation was impossible.

The TV came on to a Tampax ad, so Lilac had to frantically twiddle the knob to change the channel over. Tampax ads shouldn't be allowed. They were worse than a kissing scene that would suddenly appear in a detective show or on *Doctor Who* or something you might be watching with your dad. Jenny O'Herlihy said her annoying brother always made loud comments when there was a Tampax ad on, about how great it was that all those girls could run on a beach and go horse riding in white jeans without spilling their blue water everywhere, and Jenny said she had taken to rushing out of the room every time there was an ad break. Which made watching TV not at all a relaxing experience. Lilac wondered if maybe it was just a plot to make them all read books instead.

Jeannie wasn't paying any attention to the TV but had taken a copy of *Just Seventeen* out of her bag and was sitting down and leafing through it. Usually she had a book with her, but maybe she had decided that now she had a boyfriend she needed to be more fashionable and cool. Jeannie wasn't cool, which was one reason Lilac liked her. She seemed happy to just be who she was, not trying to impress anyone. She had a lot of brown hair that was more fuzzy than smooth, and glasses, and her jeans and jumpers were much like Lilac's jeans and jumpers – not skinny stonewashed jeans with zips on the bottom, and not big huge batwing jumpers. She wore earrings, but they weren't big plastic dangly ones, just tiny gold heart shapes. Then again, Lilac supposed that Jeannie didn't exactly dress up to go to Lilac's house, and other than that Lilac had only ever seen her in her school uniform.

'Do you wear lots of makeup when you go to discos?' Lilac heard the question come out of her mouth before she'd even thought the thought that went with it. Lilac had a sudden vision of Jeannie like Wonder Woman before her transformation, with her hair up in a bun. Then she'd shake out her hair and whip off her glasses to reveal the glamorous beauty beneath, who nobody had suspected was there all along.

'I haven't gone to a lot of discos,' said Jeannie, looking up. The good thing about Jeannie was she never minded when you asked a question out of thin air. She just answered it anyway. 'But I have a purple eyeliner. And a green one. And sparkly lip gloss. And blusher. I mostly mess around with them at home and then take it all off again before I go out anywhere.'

'Then where did you meet him if you don't go to discos?' Lilac hadn't meant to say anything about the boy, but there it was now, out in the open. She had to rejig her whole idea of how people met boyfriends if not at discos. There was of course the 'cute boy moves in next door' scenario, but that only happened in books. Nobody new ever moved in next door in real life.

'Oh.' Jeannie looked a little embarrassed. 'I didn't think you'd recognized me. I met him around Christmas. My friend Rachel's brother goes to school with him, and he had some friends over and Rachel and I were there, and I was talking to him a bit. And then weeks later he told Rachel's brother to tell Rachel that he fancied me and I told her to tell him back that I thought he was nice and then Rachel said he said I should meet him that day to go for a walk and I did and we ended up . . . well, you saw.'

'So is he your boyfriend now?'

'I don't know.' Jeannie sounded a bit forlorn. 'I forgot to give him my phone number, so I'm waiting to see if Rachel knows. She said she'd find out for me.'

'Do you want him to be your boyfriend?'

'Yeah, I suppose. He's nice. It was . . . nice.'

'Are you in love?'

'No! I don't think so. I'm not picking petals off daisies and mooning around looking all dopey and doodling my name and his together in hearts on my copybooks. So, probably, no.'

'I think if you were you'd know.'

'Yeah. I think so. It's just, like, practising.'

'OK.' Lilac had never thought of it that way before. She decided they needed a new topic of conversation because this was all getting very serious. 'It's my Confirmation tomorrow. And my birthday. Did you know? I'm turning eleven.'

'I know, you told me last time. Happy early birthday. And happy Confirmation too. What name are you taking? Are you taking the pledge? Where are you going for dinner?'

'We're going to the Swiss Chalet. Granny wants to see it because I told her it's the coolest place where everyone goes. My name is a surprise. I'll tell you next time but I can't tell you today. I think I'm taking the pledge but I might just move my lips and not actually say it. Did you take it? Do you think I should?' This conversation was much easier. Lilac felt lighter already.

'I didn't take it, but I don't want to drink, really. I just didn't want to make a promise that I wasn't sure I'd want to keep when I got a bit older. It's a long way to eighteen.'

That sounded like very sensible advice. Lilac's mum and dad said the decision to take the pledge not to drink until she was eighteen was totally up to her. She'd tasted sips of sherry and wine a few times, and it was always disgusting. Her mother said it was an acquired taste. Lilac wasn't sure why anyone would want to bother acquiring it, but it seemed like everyone did anyway.

Lilac decided to lighten the mood further by telling Jeannie the story about David Jennings's Confirmation name being Hyacinth. She carefully remembered her promise to Michael, so she didn't say who it was, just that it was a boy up the road who was her friend's brother. Jeannie thought it was very funny too. Maybe she wasn't on the other side now after all, Lilac thought. She still seemed just the same, really.

CHAPTER 16

Lilac lay in bed the next morning taking a few moments to carefully savour all the gorgeous anticipation of the day to come. There would be so much at once that if she didn't pay attention she might forget to enjoy the specialness of either her Confirmation day or her eleventh birthday. She briefly considered asking her dad to set his digital watch to beep every ten minutes, so that she could switch her focus from one thing to the other and make sure she gave them both equal time.

On her birthday morning it was traditional for her presents to be laid out on the breakfast table, so that she could admire them and open them at leisure while eating her cereal. Lilac put on her dressing gown and paraded importantly down the stairs – if you could parade while nobody else was watching. It felt like a procession, because she was going slowly to feel what it was like to go down the stairs as an eleven year old, and to make the most of the 'before' time. For these few moments, her presents could be anything at all – a bike with gears, a real bow and arrow, a pony! (Maybe not a pony on the breakfast table. A carrot signifying a pony, then.)

She turned the corner into the kitchen to be met not by applauding relatives and a pile of shiny wrapping paper, but her father and her grandmother holding forth on last night's performance at the tennis club, and her mother sitting at the table looking a little starry-eyed.

'And then,' Granny was saying to Nuala, 'I feel you started the second verse just a tiny bit off kilter, but you soon got it back, and you had the audience eating out of your hands.' Granny 'taste for the limelight' Kinsella herself seemed to be quite happy about her daughter's stage debut.

'No, that was the pianist, Tony, he almost came in at the wrong place,' Nuala replied excitedly. 'But did you see Noreen Delahunt, in the green – she walked right across in front of me just when I was coming to the high point of the song? I wanted to kick her!'

'Ah now, all this showbiz, you need a good breakfast in you to set you up for the day. We might have to beat off the paparazzi after such a performance!' Lilac's dad looked up and noticed her, finally. 'Lilac, your mum was the belle of the ball last night, she was.'

'Oh, good.' Lilac stood in the doorway wondering how to put this delicately. 'Um. My . . . birthday?'

'Oh, sweetie, I've stolen all your thunder, haven't I? I'm so sorry, do you want to go back out and read a book for a few minutes and come in again?' her mother said, flustered but ever considerate.

'No, no, it's fine.' Lilac suddenly couldn't be bothered standing on ceremony. 'I'm hungry, anyway. You didn't finish the milk, did you? Is there any nice bread left?' Presents were one thing, but breakfast was important too. 'So the musical was good?'

'It was a triumph!' said Granny, opening her arms wide as she spoke as if accepting roses being thrown from the crowd. 'There'll be notices in the paper on Monday, mark my words.'

'I don't think so, Mum,' said Nuala. She was bustling around now pulling things out of cupboards. 'Lilac, how about pancakes, since it's a special day?'

'There will. I spoke to a nice young man who said he was going to review it in the community newsletter.' Granny was emphatic. 'He took a photo.'

'Yes please for pancakes. But cereal first.' Lilac was trying hard not to ask about presents, but she did notice that her dad had slipped out of the room. She carefully kept her back to the door as she took out the Rice Krispies and got herself a bowl and spoon. She didn't want to spoil any surprises for herself.

Gerry came back in waving a piece of paper at Lilac. 'Here's the programme, look, isn't that a great shot of them all?' She looked at it, bemused. This was nothing to do with her birthday. It had a photo, from the dress rehearsal, of the tennis club ladies (and a few select gentlemen) on the stage in their costumes, and there was her mum's name at the top of the list of cast members. Lilac finally stopped being patient.

'It's my birthday! I'm eleven! I was never eleven before and now I am and nobody cares! And it's my Confirmation day which is a very important event in a young person's life and is the whole reason Granny is staying with us, and I can't believe you're not giving me any presents and you're all more interested in Mum's stupid musical!'

She stopped, wondering if running out of the room would be overdoing it, and not wanting to miss the pancakes, but unsure how else to end the scene. Guzzler saved her by coming over and nuzzling her hand, and she bent down and gave him a hug.

Without saying a word, Lilac's dad took her gently by the shoulders, straightened her up, and walked her to the back door. She looked out and saw something fuzzy and blue propped up on the patio. She wiped her eyes with her sleeve and looked again.

'The bike! With the gears! The one you said was far too expensive!' She felt a tiny bit bad about her outburst. 'Sorry for shouting. It's just, usually the presents are on the table ...' She turned back around to find that there was a big parcel sitting right in the middle of the breakfast dishes, where none had been before, and Granny was smiling like the Cheshire Cat, trying not to say 'Gotcha!'

'Your mother's not the only actress in the family,' she said, though Lilac was afraid to ask whether she was talking about everyone else's ability to pretend they'd forgotten her presents or Lilac's own tendency towards melodrama.

After pancakes, Lilac had a shower and put on her school uniform, which was a very boring thing to have to do on such a special day, she thought, but that was the rule for Confirmation. She had a brand-new uniform shirt and she had – carefully – ironed the pleats in her tunic so they were flat and crisp.

Her socks were new too, white ones that went right up to her knees instead of stopping halfway up her calves. She had insisted on the sort with in-and-out stripes, not the sort with little holes making a diamond pattern. Her mother thought she was silly, but in Lilac's mind the type of white socks you wore said a lot about you as a person. She just didn't feel like a diamond-holes-pattern girl. The other ones were much better. And her new shoes were narrow grey ones with a thin strap that you could put in front of your ankle or push over to behind the heel if you wanted real slip-ons. She used the strap, though, because otherwise they fell off. She felt quite grown-up in them, they were so unlike her usual clumpy school shoes.

She took a minute to update Margery's letter on the morning so far:

It's my birthday! Happy birthday to me! (I'm just saying it for you.) Granny gave me a real silver bracelet that I can wear today and keep for ever because it's very special. It has a tiny chain so that even when you open the catch it doesn't just fall off your wrist, because it would be terrible if I lost it. I hope nobody burgles us and steals it. Burgals? Burguls? What a strange word. It's much more serious than it looks. Anyway, nobody's allowed to steal my beautiful bracelet. It has swirly patterns on it and inside it says my name and today's date. So Granny says I'll never forget my birthday. As if I would.

CHAPTER 17

Lilac had time after lunch to continue writing her letter to Margery.

And then we went to the church and now we're at home because we're going out to dinner, not to lunch, so I have time to tell you everything.

I'm confirmed now and stuff, but Oh My God (sorry God) it was SO Embarrassing. You will not believe how embarrassing it was. I will try to tell you but you will never ever understand how it was so bad that I cannot ever go to the church again. I thought the interpretatatative dance at Easter was bad but this was much MUCH worse. The bishop went completely purple, as purple as his robe, and it was because of me.

We were all lined up as if we were going up to communion except at the top there was the bishop holding his shepherd-stick thingy — crozier, that's it — and looking very scary and bright purple — just his dress, not his face YET — and we were in alphabetical order in our classes and the boys' school went first because the girls went first last year. I heard him read out Mary when Michael got to the top and a lot of people giggled but I was really good and didn't because he's my friend and it's not his fault his Granny is mad, because not everyone can have a lovely Granny like mine.

Then we started to move slowly up the church and eventually it was Jenny Kelly right before me and he read out "Jennifer Ann" and nodded and smiled as if he thought it was very nice and appropriate and not a really boring name at all, and I thought Wait till he reads mine - it will sound even nicer and be interesting and historical as well.

Miss Grey was standing beside him with all the cards with the names on them and she whispered the name to him as each girl came up so he knew what to say. And I saw her look at my card and she sort of looked again and a funny look came over her face as if she didn't know what to do and she maybe wanted to run away but she wasn't allowed.

And then she whispered my name to the bishop and he looked all cross and muttered 'What? What?' and made her show him the card and then he shouted really loud into the microphone 'LILAC <u>SHROVE</u>?' as if he had never heard of either of those names in his life. And not as if he felt they were both beautiful names that he'd just never thought of before, either.

Of course I was struck dumb but I nodded and said 'Yes' and that was when he went really purple (and Miss Grey went a bit pink too) (and I went totally scarlet) and he said, very slowly, into the microphone so everyone could hear it all even though he was talking to me, 'SHROVE is not the name of a saint. SHROVE is the name we give to the day before Lent begins, as you very well know. You may certainly not take SHROVE as your Confirmation name. You may take Ursula. It was my mother's name. Saint Ursula was a holy virgin and a martyr. Let her life be a lesson to you.'

And then he said in a really pinchy voice: 'LILAC URSULA' and did the blessy thing with his hand and said the muttery prayer bit and put his hand on my head as if I was just any of the others and he hadn't just given out stink to me and made me take the horriblest name that was ever invented.

I hope the rest of the day gets better because as birthdays go this one is really not going well. Maybe I can be a Presbiteerian instead. They have a nice church down the road from our one.

Love, Lilac

Lilac's hand hurt from all that writing but it felt good to get it out on paper. She took a deep breath and decided she wasn't going to let the bishop ruin her birthday, even if he had ruined her entire Confirmation. From now on, they were celebrating only her birthday , and nobody was to say a word about The Other Thing. She couldn't stop saying 'Ursula! Ursula? *Ur*sula' in her head though, giving it different inflections until it had lost all meaning and was just a babble of sounds strung together. She didn't like it any better that way, though. Ursula. Nope.

CHAPTER 18

They went out early in the afternoon, Lilac wearing her
new apple-green dress from Cassidy's that had a drop
waist, with a very smart peach-coloured light jacket over it.
The weather was a bit too cold for a summer jacket, but she
didn't want to spoil the effect by adding a coat, so she
decided to just suffer. She had a little shoulder bag too, to
keep her purse and a comb and a hanky in, as her mother
said, and she felt quite a lot like an elegant young lady.

They called on several friends-of-the-family, who all
gave them tea and biscuits (or just biscuits for Lilac) and
then went to her cousins' house, where Linda was too old
and Shane was too young for Lilac to 'go off and play' with.
Lilac wished she'd brought a book. Everyone was talking to
Granny and to her mum and dad but after the first flurry of
congratulations and questions about the morning – which
Lilac ducked, as much as she could – they had nothing to
say to her. She tried to pet the cat, but it seemed he could
smell Guzzler because he would have nothing to do with
her. Or maybe he was just that sort of cat.

Lilac's Dad had planned their visiting route so that they'd get back to Stillorgan, where the Swiss Chalet was, in perfect time for dinner. The last stop was in Terenure: yet more family friends who Lilac called Uncle and Aunty but were in fact no relation. Their children were grown up and no longer lived in the house, but they had a Sodastream and a nice garden and a big dog, so Lilac always liked to see them. She perused the flavours on offer for her fizzy drink and chose blackcurrant, which was a beautiful dark shade of purple. It was nearly all gone, and Aunty Hazel, presiding over the Sodastream, said Lilac could open the new bottle of syrup and put the squirty top on it before they added it to the magically fizzied water.

Just as Lilac untwisted the metal cap on the bottle, someone opened the door from the garden and the dog bounded in, exactly the way Guzzler would, to see who these people in his house were. He must have remembered Lilac from their last visit, because he decided she was his best friend, and jumped up to greet her. The bottle of sticky, dark purple liquid tipped over and Lilac's beautiful new peach jacket and apple-green dress suddenly sprouted big wet pinkish-red splotches all down her front.

'Oh no!'

'Bad dog!'

'Down, Fionn!'

Everyone shouted in horror at the golden retriever, who was still bouncing all over the kitchen, the mud on his paws mixing with the syrup on the floor to make everything even filthier, especially Lilac, his brand-new best-ever buddy. Lilac just stood there, dripping gently, not even making a fuss, because *of course* this would happen, to ruin the birthday part of her day, after the Confirmation part of her day had already been demolished by the bishop. *Of course it would.*

They put the dog out again, with many stern words that clearly fell on happy but deaf ears. Someone picked up the bottle, which had just a dribble of syrup left in it, and wondered if Lilac still wanted her drink. Someone else produced a mop and hurriedly swiped it over the floor. Lilac didn't move. She tried hard not to cry, but the injustice of it all was beginning to get to her now that the shock had worn off, and she sniffled a little. She couldn't even blow her nose because her hanky was in her bag in the other room and she didn't want to get the bag sticky. Her mother gently removed her jacket, and dabbed at the worst of the stains on her front with a damp J-cloth that smelt faintly of dishwater. Aunty Hazel came downstairs holding a pair of navy tracksuit bottoms, which Lilac's mother took gratefully, though Lilac wasn't so sure.

'It's lucky Aoife left these in her room; I think they'll fit, and if they're too long, sure they're elasticated at the bottom so that'll keep them from dragging on the floor. I couldn't find a T-shirt, though . . .'

Granny said, 'I have just the thing! Providence must have caused me to bring your last present with us instead of giving it to you at home, Lilac. Here you are!' Then she realised that anything Lilac touched was still going to encounter purple stickiness, so instead of handing Lilac the large gift-wrapped object she had just produced from her capacious handbag (as she always called it), she opened it herself and proudly unfolded a vision of fluffy black mohair with gold bobbles all over it. The jumper. Granny had really outdone herself on this one, Lilac thought. It was spectacularly horrible.

'I thought the black would be very sophisticated now that you're a bit older, even though in general I think black on young people looks quite funereal.' Lilac's mum and Aunty Hazel nodded in agreement. 'But the gold bobbles are a bit of fun, don't you think? Helen McArdle taught me how to do them; I think I'll be putting them on everything now.' She was delighted to be the provider of the right thing at exactly the right time.

Lilac swallowed hard. Her mum shepherded her to the downstairs loo, put the tracksuit bottoms and the jumper on the cistern, and said, 'I'll leave you to change, sweetie. Try not to get purple on the towel, won't you?'

'I think,' Lilac said to Agatha at school on Monday, 'it's meant to be one of those things where people look back on it afterwards and laugh about how funny it was. Except it wasn't funny and I will never look back on it that way.'

Agatha nodded sympathetically and said, 'It must have been awful.'

'You cannot even imagine,' Lilac agreed sadly. 'There wasn't time to go home and change because our dinner booking was for seven o'clock and it was already half past six and we were way over there on the other side of Stillorgan, wherever Terenure is, miles and miles from here anyway. So I wore navy tracksuit bottoms that were too big and a fluffy black jumper with gold bobbles all over it to the Swiss Chalet for the special dinner I'd been looking forward to for so long.'

'Did you see anyone you knew?'

'I stared at the ground the whole way in from the car until we sat down. Then I took a quick look around and thought maybe I saw Angela Delaney with her family but I looked away really quickly.'

'Maybe it wasn't her.'

'I hope not. And I really needed to go to the loo after drinking my Coke float, but I couldn't walk past all the other tables looking like that so I just held it in.'

'Were the chicken and chips nice? And the coleslaw?'

'I don't like coleslaw but Mum said it was. My chips were nice but I was mostly thinking about how I needed to wee, so I'm not sure about the chicken.'

'Did you have pudding?'

'Granny and I shared a banana split. It was really good. I gave the glacé cherry to my dad because nobody else likes them. I think he only eats them so they won't go to waste.'

'How can anyone like glacé cherries? I don't know why they even put them on things.'

'Maybe there's some country where all they grow is glacé cherries and all the other countries feel sorry for it and have to buy them so that country won't be poor and have a famine.'

'But they could eat their own glacé cherries so they wouldn't have a famine.'

'They probably don't like them either.'

Global economics was very complicated. Lilac started to feel a little more hopeful, though. She was pretty sure that between Easter and this weekend, she had gone through everything embarrassing that could ever happen. Life could only get better.

CHAPTER 19

Granny went back to Cork on Sunday evening. She was flying to Nepal on Wednesday, so she had some packing to do.

'*Why* did you have to move to Cork, Granny?' Lilac asked plaintively on the way to the station. 'We miss you. And wouldn't it be much easier to fly out of Dublin for all your travelling?'

'Ah, wusha now, child,' said Granny, putting on a fake Irishy accent that wasn't her real one at all. 'Shannon's just as good to fly out of, and easier to get to with all the traffic up here. I like the pace of life down there, and the regatta.'

Granny never did properly answer Lilac's questions about why she had moved, which made Lilac think all the more that she really was a spy, or a secret agent or something. Maybe her travels were actually top-secret missions for the government, like James Bond. Only less dangerous, of course. All the colourful scarves might be for tying up criminals so she could deliver them into the hands of the law.

Granny gave Lilac an extra big hug before she stepped up into the train, her bags and baggage already in the luggage rack and only one scarf (bright blue, woollen, large) swathed around her shoulders almost like a cloak, because the carriages were cold sometimes. Lilac hugged back, so tight she had to close her eyes. She felt a kiss on the top of her head, and then Granny was away up the steps and sitting comfortably by the window, rummaging in her bag for her book to put on the table in front of her, before the train began to pull out and they all waved like mad at each other.

Lilac ran along the platform beside Granny's window until the train went too fast. Then she stopped, panting, watching until the very end had gone around the corner out of the station and everything was quiet again. She turned and walked back up to Gerry, and they drove home feeling that it had been a very long and busy Easter holidays.

When Lilac got home from school on Monday, after she'd decided to never think of her eleventh birthday again, she found a little package from Margery in the post. Inside, there was a lovely card with a picture of a pony, and a tiny present beautifully wrapped in tissue paper with a thin piece of ribbon around it. Lilac decided to save the present till last, so first she unfolded the letter that was inside the card.

Dear Eleven-Year-Old Lilac, The Birthday Girl,

I am so so so so (x 100,000) sorry that this is probably going to arrive late. I was planning so carefully and I had your present ready yonks ago but I put it away to keep it safe and then I nearly forgot. I can't believe you're eleven. Well, yes, I suppose I can because I feel nearly eleven too. Just give me two months to catch up.

When Caroline was eleven I was only five. There's a photo of us together on summer holidays in Wexford in the rain and she looks really tall. I don't think I'm that tall. Maybe it's just because she was wearing huge big bell-bottoms like from the 70s. Her hair looked as if someone had put a bowl on her head and cut around it. Mum says it was a page-boy style and very fashionable just then but I don't think it was a good look on Caroline.

Caroline says she's on a diet so she won't eat dinner these nights. But then she goes to the mall with her friends and they have this competition where they take turns to sit down beside someone in the food court who's just about to eat a pizza slice. They start talking to them about how unhealthy all that cheese is, until the person walks away and leave their food behind. She says they're doing it for the people's own good, and that they're exploring their powers of perswashion because they want

94

to go into politics. But then even if the person has already taken a bite out of it, Caroline and her friends eat the rest of their pizza. Whoever gets the most pizza wins. And they have to buy everyone else ice cream.

Mum thinks Caroline is going to fade away because of all the missed dinners, but Caroline says I'm not allowed tell her about the mall thing in case they get in trouble. She doesn't look like she's fading away, anyway, because she's winning the pizza competition. She only told me about it because she had to borrow my money to buy the ice cream last night.

I have to go to Tim Horton's with Dad now because we're going to post this on the way back. Happy happy birthday and I hope you like your present. (But don't get too excited about it if you haven't opened it yet.)

Love from Margery

P.S. Read the note.
P.P.S. I'm putting in an extra thing too.

Lilac wondered who Tim Horton was. Then something else fluttered out of the card. She picked it up and found she was looking at a photograph that was somehow familiar – because she'd just read its description in Margery's letter. Even though it was raining in the picture, the colours were extra yellowy. Caroline looked like herself but strange at the same time because of the hair and the clothes. Margery looked like a cute little five-year-old in a flowery dress and a raincoat and wellies, and she was smiling, but Caroline in hugely flared jeans and a polo neck was scowling and rolling her eyes up to heaven at the same time, as if she couldn't believe her parents were insisting on taking this stupid photograph.

Lilac turned it over and saw that as well as the faded writing in the top corner that said 'Rosslare, Aug. '81', there was a new bit in Margery's writing that said 'Mum said I could have the photo, because Caroline hates it so much she won't mind. Caroline was annoyed in it because she wouldn't wear her anorak and then she got wet. I remember it exactly.'

Then Lilac unwrapped the present. It was a very pretty pebble, pinkish with white lines running through it. Part of the wrapping had another note written on it.

Caroline keeps borrowing my pocket money for things she says she absolutely needs. She hasn't paid me back yet so I can't buy you a present, but I found this and I knew you'd like it. xxx ooo M.

She was right, Lilac did like it.

CHAPTER 20

'Have you noticed,' Lilac asked Agatha at school on Tuesday in a stage whisper, 'that Miss Grey is acting a bit strangely?'

'Now you mention it,' said Agatha, pretending to think very hard, 'there *is* something a little odd about her.'

Miss Grey was sitting at her desk talking to herself. She had two pencils stuck in her hair, which was up in a messy bun. She was wearing a nice skirt, but on her top half she had a zipped-up tracksuit top with what looked like cat hairs on it. She looked paler than usual because she wasn't wearing her usual pink lipstick and blusher. And she hadn't looked up once since they had come into the room that morning. The noise levels were rising, but Miss Grey was frantically sorting through sheets of paper and muttering, oblivious to the class.

'Miss Grey!' Lilac tried calling in a low voice, from her desk near the front. 'Earth to Miss Grey!' She didn't want to startle her. Miss Grey looked even more like a nervous woodland creature than usual.

Miss Grey looked up, and took a moment to focus on Lilac through her large-framed glasses. 'Oh. Oh, sorry girls – is that the time already?' Evidently it was, since all twenty-four of them were at their desks. (All except for Theresa Quirke and Maura Rooney, who were having a sword fight with the broom handle and the dustpan. They put them down and sat in their places.) Miss Grey looked down at her red tracksuit top and quickly unzipped it to reveal a blouse that looked much more appropriate with the skirt. She bundled the top into one of her desk drawers, took a pale green cardigan off the back of her chair, and stood up, smoothing her hair and removing the pencils as her hands encountered them. 'I'm trying to sort out the seating plan for my wedding reception. It's . . . tricky,' she explained.

'My aunty got married last year,' Laura Devine volunteered. 'My mam said it'd be a miracle if they were all still standing by the time she got to the altar because she was like a headless chicken with all the organizing. Are you like that?' she asked sympathetically.

'Can we help?' asked Agatha. Lilac thought Agatha was bonkers to offer, as if they could do anything to help in planning a wedding, but Agatha had a soft heart.

'No, no, not at all –' Miss Grey started to say, but then she changed her mind. 'You know, maybe you could, girls. I was just thinking that the whole thing is like a complicated logic problem. Certain people have to sit together and others have to be kept apart, and we have to have exactly eight tables of ten people each.'

The class was ecstatic. To get to help with real wedding-planning! Maybe they could decide on a menu – a colour scheme – bridesmaids' dresses – they all started talking at once. 'I think peach for the flower girls, don't you?' Katie Byrne said across the table to Agatha and Lilac. 'Or maybe li . . . lavender.' She had been going to say 'lilac' but changed her mind out of politeness, in case Lilac didn't like being reduced to a mere colour.

An hour later they all had name badges and had rearranged the desks into eight groups. There weren't enough of them to impersonate all eighty guests, and of course there weren't eighty chairs, but they made pencil cases and lunch boxes stand in for the rest of the guests and put name badges on those too. These were the straightforward ones, like Miss Grey herself and her fiancé and the bridesmaids and groomsmen, who would all be at the 'top table'. Most of Miss Grey's friends and her fiancé's friends fit nicely between three tables.

It was the uncles and aunts and her parents' friends and her fiancé's parents' friends who were causing the 'um . . . difficulties', as Miss Grey put it, and so some of the name badges had extra information underneath. Lilac had half a page of instructions pinned to her front:

Uncle John (bride's side):
- *Needs to sit far from the bar, drinks like a fish*
- *Must avoid groom's aunts*
- *Must be near bride's mother (to keep an eye on him)*
- *Allergic to flowers*
- *Not near mortal enemy Uncle Tadhg (groom's side)*
- *Obsessed with weather – sit away from Matt P, the meteorologist*

Agatha had something similar, but hers read

Terry P:
- *Must sit at different table from her husband, Liam P.*
- *Must be near Mary F. or she'll just move there anyway*
- *Sit far from the band because she'll complain about the music being too loud*
- *Child-free table; swears like a sailor*

Miss Grey was using initials instead of surnames, just in case anyone in the class happened to know any of the guests. Lilac thought that was very unlikely. There were fifteen guests in particular with varying levels of difficulty who had to be distributed around the tables in just the right way. The blackboard was the bar, they decided, and the library shelves at the end of the classroom were where the band would be.

By lunchtime they were pretty sure they had it right. Miss Grey had spent a long time saying things like 'You go over there beside Seán Mc . . . oh, no wait, you can't be there – here then, back where you started, but switch with Ruth O', and now she was finally satisfied.

'Nobody move!' she announced, while she started drawing up the final diagram in her giant red notebook with the wire spiral and putting all the names in the right places. 'Girls, thank you so much for helping me with this. I don't know how I'd have done it without you. And I think we've definitely practised some logical thinking, don't you?' Lilac wasn't so sure about that, but it had certainly made a change from fractions and decimals.

'Maybe tomorrow,' said Adele Duffy, ever the optimist, 'we can help you choose the bridesmaids' dresses.'

'Maybe,' said Miss Grey; but it was the sort of maybe that really meant 'not a chance'. The next day she had her lipstick firmly in place and they spent all morning learning about the *Modh Coinníollach*.

CHAPTER 21

Dear Margery,

Guess who turns out to be Jeannie's boyfriend-type-person? Michael's brother David from up the road!!! I can't believe I didn't figure it out sooner because it's so obvious. She said he lived near here, and Michael said David had a new girlfriend, but no, I still had to go and get myself into trouble by opening my big mouth and talking, just like I always do.

Because Michael told me his brother's confirmation name was Hyacinth and I happened to tell Jeannie the story about how I knew someone whose brother's confirmation name was Hyacinth, without mentioning any names (except the name Hyacinth, obviously, because it would be a pretty bad story if I left that out). And THEN Jeannie said it to her boyfriend — I don't know why they were talking about Confirmation names unless it's because my turning-the-bishop-purple incident is still the talk of the town — and he laughed in this really weird way, she said, and then he wouldn't talk to her, and then finally he admitted it was him.

I had NO IDEA or obviously I'd never have told her, but nobody listens to me when I try to explain. So David's angry with Michael and Michael's angry with me and Jeannie thinks he might break up with her even though she wasn't quite sure yet that they were actually going out together, and it wasn't my fault.

Confirmation names are nothing but trouble. You're really lucky you don't have to do it yet. Maybe they'll forget and just never have you make your Confirmation at all. I don't see how it would matter. It's not as if you need to prove it for anything. Until you get to Heaven, maybe, but I'm not sure they can keep you out. You could say they lost the paperwork. They're always losing paperwork here, I bet they have loads of it in Heaven.

Thank you for the present, I love it. And the photo. I love that too. I will mind it carefully and never let Jeannie see it, because I think she knows Caroline from school.

Who is Tim Horton and why did you go to his house? Is he Caroline's new boyfriend?

Love from
Lilac Who Is Eleven But Not Any Better At Keeping Her Mouth Shut

Lilac was really annoyed with Michael for thinking it was her fault. After all, he was the one who told her about David's name in the first place. He should have kept his own big mouth shut.

Dear Lilac,

Tim Horton's is a coffee shop that sells yummy doughnuts too. I think it's really funny that you thought maybe it was Caroline's new boyfriend's name.

The food court people saw what Caroline and her friends were doing with the pizzas and now they're banned from the mall. Now they spend all their time at Tim Horton's, so it's as if he is her new boyfriend, actually. I don't know if they're telling people that doughnuts are bad for them and then stealing those, but they might be.

She's eating dinner again so Mum is happier, but now Mum has decided we should be vegetarians so it's all nut loaf and lentil casserole and mushroom ragoo. Caroline's weird so she likes that stuff. Dad has started going to Tim Horton's a lot more too, though. I mostly just eat lunch from the cafeteria at school and then an apple for dinner.

Did I tell you about the cafeteria at school? We can get chips and burgers and pizza slices and fish fingers and chicken nuggets and lasagne and they're all really cheap. It's practically McDonald's. I may never be able to go back to cheese sandwiches and a Club Milk after this.

I wish I didn't have to miss your party, though. I'd eat sandwiches if I got to go to it. And Club Milks are pretty nice really. I hope you have a really good time and the new girl is not awful.

Love from Margery

Lilac was confused for a minute about the food court at the mall. She had an image in her head of a judge in a wig and Caroline in handcuffs being sent to prison by the food court, but then she remembered it was just what they called the place with all the food in the shopping center. Margery had mentioned it before. All these things were so normal to Margery now that she forgot to explain them sometimes, even though a few months ago she had never heard of them either.

Lilac sometimes worried that Margery would be so

different and Canadian when she came back next summer that they wouldn't be friends again. Maybe everything in Ireland would look small and silly now that Margery had lived in Ontario, which was practically beside California, and California was probably the coolest place in the world. Lilac wasn't sure she could live up to the pressure.

Maybe Margery would have to be friends with Teresa Quirke and the cool girls in the class instead, with their stone-washed jeans with patches and their giant sweatshirts that were not woolly jumpers knitted by their grannies. They always tossed their heads so their hair flipped over exactly when Lilac was passing, as if she was so uncool they didn't even want to have to see her. Lilac's hair was too curly to flip – it just bounced back to where it always was, no matter how often she practiced in front of the mirror.

Lilac had decided to use the photo Margery had sent her as a bookmark, because that way she'd be able to admire it regularly and she would never lose it. Lilac was very careful with bookmarks because she hated having to flick through a book to find the place she'd been. And she always took her book to school in case she had some free time, so she couldn't just leave it face down at the open page beside her bed. Anyway, it was bad to do that to library books.

CHAPTER 22

'So what are we doing for my party, Mum?' Lilac asked over dinner. 'Or is it a secret? Should I not ask?'

'Your party? Is that this weekend? Do we not get a weekend off from high jinks and celebrations, ever?' asked her father in mock surprise. At least, Lilac hoped it was mock. For a moment, she feared the worst: these were the parents who made her shop for her own Easter egg, after all. Had they forgotten her party too?

'Hmm', said her mother. 'I don't know if I should let you in on it or keep it to myself. Which would you rather?'

'I think I'd prefer to know, please,' said Lilac, relieved that there was something in train, at least. 'In case I need to, well, *adjust* anything.' What she meant was, in case you've planned something horribly embarrassing that I wouldn't even have liked when I was seven. 'I was going to wear my blue dress with the stripes and the little white belt. But not if we're going hiking or something. Not that I want to go hiking,' she added hastily. Hiking was not an acceptable party activity. In fact, most people in her class seemed to do the cinema-trip-plus-McDonald's thing for their parties, but Lilac didn't really want to do that. She didn't even like burgers.

'Well, we've got, how many girls? Six, was it?'

Lilac counted them off on her fingers: 'Me, Agatha, Jenny O, Katie Byrne, Naomi' – Naomi was a friend from outside school; she and Lilac only saw each other at their birthday parties these days, but they were still friends – 'and Evelyn,' she ended, heaving a put-upon sigh.

'She's a perfectly lovely girl, I'm sure, and you'll all get along great guns.'

Lilac made a face at her mother's expression: 'great guns' – who would even say that? – and then looked up again. 'You're *sure*? You've never even *met* her? You invited a girl you've never even seen to my party, just because you felt bad about beating her mum at tennis?'

'Who told you I beat her at tennis? I may have knocked her out of the round robin by two sets to love' – Nuala tried not to look like the cat who'd got the cream, but didn't succeed – 'but that's neither here nor there. I just thought Evelyn might like to make some new friends, since her family is new to the area.'

'Making friends isn't the same as just meeting people the same age,' Lilac said gloomily. 'Not any more. But six of us, yes.'

'Well, we can fit six in the car. Four across the back and two in the boot. Or five in the back and one in the boot. You can sit on each other's knees, you're all quite petite. So I thought we'd go somewhere nice.'

'Nice how?' Lilac was suspicious. 'What sort of nice?'

'Well, it depends on the weather. But probably a little scavenger hunt on the beach, and then afternoon tea with buns at the bakery in the village. Do you think that would work?'

That sounded . . . not too bad. That could actually be quite nice, Lilac thought. 'Is there a prize for the scavenger hunt? What will we scavenge for?'

'Ah, now that would be telling,' said Gerry with a big grin. 'What's for pudding? Is that a rhubarb tart I spy there? Custard or ice cream?'

CHAPTER 23

The party was to be at three on Saturday afternoon. They would spend about two hours at the beach and then go to the bakery for tea at five. 'Tea' wouldn't be actual tea, of course, but maybe hot chocolate if they were cold from the beach, or fizzy drinks, and buns or scones or perhaps those delicious caramel squares with shortbread underneath and chocolate on top. Lilac was planning on one of those.

Nuala had reserved two tables for the party, which was not the normal sort of thing to do in the little bakery café that was just off the main street, but she told them it was a special occasion and they had been happy to help, even though Saturday afternoon was one of their busiest times, they said. She assured them that the party would arrive on time and would eat lots of delicious bakery treats, so it would be worth their while.

Naomi arrived first, because she was coming the furthest. Her mum was an old friend of Lilac's mother from before they were both married, so they arrived before lunch and stayed to eat quiche and salad that Nuala had gone to quite some trouble over.

'I was so pleased that I had arranged the whole party to be out of the house so I wouldn't have to clean anything or cook anything, and then I go and invite Olivia to lunch so I have to do it anyway,' she said, exasperated with herself. But Naomi's mum, Olivia, was never the sort of person to mind a little mess or be picky about what you gave her to eat. She had a big laugh and a big hug and lots of stories to tell, and she arrived with a bottle of red wine – 'at lunchtime, no less, but a drop won't hurt,' said Gerry as he rummaged for the corkscrew.

Lilac and Naomi made themselves toasted cheese sandwiches that were crunchy outside and gooey inside and much nicer, they thought, than squishy quiche with mushrooms in it. Much like their mothers, the two girls hardly ever saw each other, but usually found it easy to slip back into their old comfortable friendship after the first few minutes of strangeness.

Lilac had plenty to talk about, as she had to bring Naomi up to date on who else would be at the party. Naomi had met Margery the year before, but of course Margery wasn't here now. Agatha was new because she'd only moved to town last summer, and Lilac hadn't been friends enough with Katie Byrne or Jenny O to invite them last year either. And then there was the dreaded Evelyn, the unknown quantity. Naomi said they should give her the benefit of the doubt.

'Well, I will,' Lilac agreed magnanimously. 'But Mum hasn't even met her herself. She could be . . . could be . . .'

'*What* could she be, though? What's the worst possible

outcome here?' Sometimes Naomi sounded a bit like a teacher. 'A space alien?' They both giggled at the thought of Evelyn with antennae and scaly green legs.

'I'd like to meet a space alien. But no, she could be really rich and snooty like those girls at the private school. She might wear T-shirts with collars and the little alligator on them.'

'I have one of those T-shirts,' said Naomi, looking a little injured. Naomi was tall and tanned, with thick swingy blonde hair that was layered at the sides, and in some ways she looked very much like those girls who went to the private school.

'Oh.' Lilac scrambled to dig herself back out of that hole. 'But you're nice. I just mean she might be not nice and wear those T-shirts as well. All the time. Sometimes, girls with those sort of clothes are kind of snobby, you know? Other girls, I mean . . .' She trailed off and looked around for a new topic of conversation.

'Did you know Guzzler nearly died before Christmas? He got lost and then he got knocked down and his leg was broken. A lady found him and took him to the vet and we were out calling for him all over the town and finally we met her. It was very dramatic. Poor puppy.' Guzzler was fast asleep on his bed, twitching gently, but Lilac ran over to quickly fluff his ears and kiss his nose. He woke up with a start, pulled out of his doggie dream; once he saw who it was, he resigned himself and closed his eyes again patiently.

Naomi wasn't a big fan of dogs, but she looked sympathetic and made polite noises about how awful it must have been. The awkward T-shirt moment passed, and the subject of Evelyn was left behind.

A little before three, they set off in the car to pick up the other girls. Gerry was driving, Nuala was in the front seat, and Naomi and Lilac were in the back. Nuala looked at the space left in the back seat a little doubtfully, but Gerry said 'Plenty of room!' and 'Glad we have a hatchback!'

Agatha was first on the list. She sat in beside Lilac, who made some quick introductions. Agatha had been as well primed on who Naomi was as Naomi had been on Agatha, so they nodded and smiled and said hi. They all giggled about the squash that was about to begin, with two more people to fit on a seat that was mostly full already.

Jenny O and Katie Byrne were both at Jenny's house. Lilac clambered over the back seat into the boot, where there was plenty of space so long as she didn't want to sit up straight or stretch out her legs. The back seat was as full as it could get now, with Katie sitting half on Agatha and half on Naomi. Nuala had presents piled up on her lap; they'd forgotten about needing space for those, but luckily nobody seemed to have given Lilac a game of Monopoly or a giant stuffed panda bear or anything else that might take up a lot of space. Lilac craned her neck from the back of the car to see what shapes the various wrapping papers might be covering, but it was impossible to tell.

Gerry said sternly that he couldn't possibly drive with all this noisy giggling, but Lilac could hear a smile in his voice. The noisy giggling turned into stifled giggling and the occasional snort, probably just as distracting. 'I hope nobody farts,' Katie whispered, and everyone tried so hard not to laugh out loud that they squeaked and squawked instead. Naomi didn't seem to be worried by the fact that all the other girls knew each other already, and she had started tickling Katie, who had no room to squirm away.

'Last but not least,' announced Nuala as they pulled up outside a house with big gates and a high wall. 'Now girls, be extra nice to Evelyn, because she's new to the area.' She looked with dismay at the back of the car. 'Where is she going to fit? Have you all been growing?'

'There's room for one more back here,' Lilac volunteered. 'It's not for long; just as far as the cove, right?'

'Well, I don't think we can ask Evelyn to squeeze in there beside you, Lilac. Naomi, maybe you would do it, might you? Thank you, sweetie.' Nuala knew Naomi best of all the other girls: she'd been coming to Lilac's birthdays since she was a year old. In the summer sometimes Naomi came to stay for days at a time and was temporarily part of the family. Practically speaking, Agatha might have been a better choice as she was the smallest of all the girls in the car, but Naomi was happy enough to oblige.

Everyone rearranged themselves with much flailing of limbs and unnecessary turning around, and Nuala got out of the front seat to greet Evelyn and her mother, who were just coming out of the gate with a youngish man in a tweed cap who seemed to be great friends with everyone. For a moment Lilac stared at him, trying to remember where she'd seen him before and why he gave her a cold, crawly feeling, and then she remembered that he was the man who had been petting Guzzler outside the supermarket when she bought her Easter egg. She shook her head to dislodge the icky feeling, and brought her attention back to the new girl.

While the mothers talked, Evelyn waited patiently by the back door of the car for a space to become apparent. One didn't, really, but she gamely ducked her head into the car and sat herself on the nearest pair of knees anyway before anyone had really had a chance to take her in.

From the back, Lilac could see that Evelyn had short choppy black hair – so black it was somehow almost purple – and two little stud earrings in her left ear. She was wearing a black T-shirt with a black cardigan over it, and when Lilac craned her neck she could see that one knee of Evelyn's grey jeans had a rip going right across it. Nuala said goodbye to Evelyn's mum, sat back into the passenger seat, and turned around to tell Evelyn who was who. Lilac saw a funny look on her mother's face, but she couldn't quite tell what it meant. She watched the back of Evelyn's head nodding at each name, and then it turned around as much as it could – which wasn't much, given the squeeze of people on the back seat – to say hi to Lilac and Agatha behind her. She had a shy friendly smile and a lot of black eyeliner.

Lilac gasped. She hadn't meant to, but she couldn't help it. 'You're a punk!' she said, half delighted and half terrified. Evelyn was so different from what Lilac had pictured, so far from the snobby Lacoste-wearing posh girl of her imagination, and so much not how an Evelyn sounded as if she would be, that Lilac was having trouble knowing what to think. She had spent so much time planning how she would defend herself against the imaginary Evelyn, who would look snootily down her nose at Lilac and her uncool friends – but she couldn't even begin to think how they all looked to this real and very different Evelyn.

Evelyn didn't seem offended. 'I prefer being called Ev,' she said, 'but my mum always insists on saying Evelyn. My brother's a real punk. He lives in London and he has a huge pink and blue mohawk. I'm more of a Curehead.'

Nobody was quite sure what a Curehead was, so they didn't pursue that one. 'And your mum lets you wear makeup?' Jenny O asked in delight, even though the answer was obviously yes.

'I don't wear it to school, and she says she doesn't mind how I look at the weekend so long as I'm happy. I have two big brothers and a little sister, so I mostly fly under the radar, parent-wise.' She spoke in a soft voice, because obviously that wasn't the sort of thing you normally said in front of anyone else's parents either. Luckily, Gerry and Nuala were having a discussion in the front about just how many people it was legal to have in a medium-sized hatchback, and had stopped listening to the girls' conversation.

'Sure it's no distance to the cove anyway,' said Gerry, decisively. 'If I'm nippy nobody will even see us.' He put the pedal to the floor and the car lurched off. 'Must watch the steering,' he muttered. 'It's a bit less responsive than usual.' Nuala put a hand out towards the steering wheel as if to help him, then took it back gingerly and gripped her handbag instead.

CHAPTER 24

They weren't going to the 'seafront' – the wide stony beach that everyone who lived in town knew well. That wouldn't be special at all. 'The cove' was a little further down the coast: one of the many little curves in the land that made a secluded and perfectly crescent-shaped beach. The weather was in-betweeny, with the sun constantly going behind clouds and rain almost threatening, but so far the drops had held off; and it wasn't too cold. Most of the girls wore light jackets and runners, because they'd been told about the plan.

Gerry parked at the side of the road, in a tiny lay-by where the grass verge was just a little wider than nonexistent, and they all tumbled out of the car like more rabbits than you would have imagined could fit in a magician's hat. There was a thin gap in the hedge if you knew where to look, and a faint track across the field. Then with a hop, a skip and a jump – as Lilac's mum put it – down the shallow cliffy bit, they found themselves in the hidden cove, with big stones at the top, then pebbles, and finally pale brown sand at the water's edge. The tide was out and a line of lumpy bladderwrack and other frondy, feathery seaweed showed how far up the water had come six hours earlier.

At each side of the cove, big rocks covered with yellow lichen held pools of wonders – deep purple waving anemones that would clump up into a jelly eyeball as soon as you touched them, delicate shrimp that were almost transparent, periwinkles that you could collect and take home to climb up the sides of a bucket, crabs ranging from the size of your hand to the size of your fingernail.

This was Lilac's family's secret place. They didn't own the cove, of course – nobody did – but they felt as if they were the only people who knew about it. They would come here on a summer bank holiday weekend when Killiney Beach to the north and Brittas Bay to the south were thronged with people, and there might be three other families here at most. Guzzler loved it more than any other beach – although they'd had to leave him at home today because there would be no room in the car. There had been some debate about bringing the party here, because Lilac didn't want word getting out about the cove, but in the end she decided it was such a perfect place for a scavenger hunt that she'd like to show it off to her friends.

Gerry paired them up in teams – Lilac and Agatha, Jenny and Katie, Naomi and Ev – and gave them each a sealed envelope and a plastic bucket and spade. In the envelope was a list of ten things to find; some were the same as the other teams' things and some were different. The first team back with all their items would win a prize. Lilac was impressed: the envelopes were colour-coordinated with the buckets, and on each one Gerry had drawn a little cartoon of a group of girls on a beach. Nuala spread a picnic blanket on one of the biggest boulders near the top of the shingle, arranged herself and her things there, and took out the camera. She was the official family commemorator of birthdays and other important events. Even though Gerry was the artist, he had a bad track record with cameras.

Gerry stood each team facing in a different direction (nobody was facing directly into the sea, though) and then, with a dramatic flourish as if he was waving an invisible bullfighter's cape, he sent them off to open their envelopes and start the collecting.

Lilac and Agatha ran to the nearest rocks, on the right-hand side of the beach. Lilac ripped open their green envelope and together they scanned the list – seaweed bubble, anemone (flower), pure white pebble, razor shell, gold coin . . . Lilac lifted her head. 'Dad! Gold coins? We're not pirates!'

'Just look for everything on your list,' said Gerry unflappably, as if it was perfectly reasonable to expect to find gold coins in rock pools. By the look of it, Naomi and Ev were having the same sort of conversation with Lilac's mum up at the back of the beach. 'Maybe they're meant to find an eye patch and a parrot,' Lilac said, pointing them out to Agatha. Jenny and Katie were already busy clambering over the rocks at the other side of the beach, peering into crevices and poking at things with their plastic shovels.

Industrious searching prevailed for a while, the girls calling to each other as they found and discarded things, or forgot what was on the list, or had something to put in the team bucket. Some of the items were so easy to find it was just a case of scanning the area – seaweed with a bubble in it, a pink flower from the grass above the cliffs – but others, like the razor shell and a crab, required quite a lot of dedicated searching and even digging. Agatha found a stash of gold-foil-covered chocolate coins hidden between the rocks almost where they met the cliff. 'Pirates, my eye!' crowed Lilac in delight. 'Pieces of eight!'

Suddenly, there was a shriek and a splash from the other side of the cove, and everyone ran to see what had happened. Ev appeared sheepishly, her top half dripping.

'I was going after a prawn and I leaned too far over,' she said, trying to wring out her black cardigan while she was still wearing it. Nuala came down from her boulder onto the pebbles and fussed over Ev like a mother hen.

'Oh dear, how unfortunate, and I didn't even bring a towel. I don't want to bring you back to your mother with pneumonia. Lilac, run up to the car and see if my jumper is in the big bag in front of the passenger seat.'

Lilac came back a few minutes later with a fluffy pink item that looked more closely related to a rabbit than a piece of clothing, thinking that only her parents would plan a trip to the beach with everything they could possibly need except a towel. Nuala brought Ev behind the rocks where there was a sheltered half-cave and told the others that everything was under control and to go back to their hunting.

When Ev emerged for a second time, she looked even more sheepish than she had after she'd fallen in, because baby-pink angora was not the sort of thing she'd usually wear. Nuala clearly approved. 'It brings out your brown eyes beautifully, Evelyn,' she was saying, 'and your delicate skin tone. You might think of trying a deep brown hair dye instead of the black some time, just for a change. I think it would really suit your colouring.'

'Did you know Ev's hair was dyed?' Agatha asked Lilac in a whisper, overhearing this as they sorted through pebbles on the stony part of the beach looking for one that might have been glass a long time ago.

'I hadn't really thought about it,' said Lilac. 'You don't expect girls our age to have dyed hair, I suppose.'

'But she's really nice,' Agatha added hastily. 'I like her.'

'So do I. She's . . . really not what I was expecting,' said Lilac, trying to remember what the Evelyn she'd worried about had looked like, the one with the Lacoste shirts and the snooty attitude. It seemed like an idea from a long time ago, even though it had only been that morning.

Ev went back to join Naomi, who was still trying to finish up their list. Nuala spread Ev's wet cardigan and T-shirt out on the big rocks to dry a little. Gerry was passing the time skimming flat pebbles into the sea. A little while later a jubilant shout went up from Katie and Jenny as they found the last item on their list – a tiny plastic parrot, in fact – and declared themselves the winners.

Lilac insisted on taking off her shoes and socks and having a ceremonial paddle, even though the April-cold sea turned her feet a delicate shade of purple. The others did not join in, and Ev was really quite chilly after her accidental dip, in spite of the pink angora, so the prize-giving ceremony was brief. Gerry counted out each item from Katie and Jenny's bucket to make sure there'd been no cheating, and solemnly declared them the victors. They were presented with a tiny painting each, a miniature showing a single pink anemone bobbing in the wind, on a real canvas. Everyone else got to share the chocolate coins that had been Lilac and Agatha's mystery object.

'This is the best prize I've ever won!' Katie said, thrilled with her own personal painting, and Lilac had to admit that having a dad who was a real artist was quite good. Sometimes, mostly when she was around people who were like the imaginary Evelyn had been, Lilac thought she'd prefer to have a dad with a boring job in the bank or at an office. She might have wished the prize was a more normal shop-bought thing like a book token or a bar of chocolate. Not today, though. Today, she was secretly quite proud of her dad. She snuck up behind him and gave him a hug, and he reached an arm around and hugged her back.

CHAPTER 25

Then they all piled into the car again and drove back to town where, as promised, the tiny bakery had reserved two tables for them. Nuala wouldn't hear of Ev putting her damp clothes back on, so Ev kept her head very low and avoided eye contact with anyone in case she might see someone who knew her. Lilac could see that Ev was being polite but dying on the inside, so she and Agatha walked close in front of her and gave her the corner chair so that she could sit unobserved by most of the general public.

Because Lilac had so recently found herself in a very similar situation, after the Sodastream incident, she felt as if she could see Ev's experience from the inside and the outside at the same time. She knew exactly how awful Ev was feeling, but could also see that – as her mum had tried to tell her at the time – everyone really wasn't staring at her and wondering how she could possibly wear that, because hardly anyone noticed.

Sticky buns and hot chocolates were ordered by all, and the six girls crowded around one small table while Gerry and Nuala sat and sipped their tea at the other, pretending not to be with them unless the laughter got too raucous. Then the lights were dimmed and a cake with 'Happy Birthday Lilac' written on it in blue icing was brought out, and they all sang and Lilac shrank down in her chair, delighted and mortified in equal measure to have this going on in a public place. The old ladies at the third table looked on with smiles and magnanimous waves of the hand, and Lilac decided maybe she'd brought a little sunshine into their drab lives.

'You're clashing with your dress,' Katie said to her, because Katie was never one to kindly ignore blushes until they went away. 'You're pinker than Ev's jumper.' Ev glowered at Katie, but in a friendly way, not an 'I'll send my brother to your house to murder you' one. Probably not, at least.

Eventually they were all as stuffed full of cake and other sweet things as they could be, and it was time to let other customers use the café tables. They all wedged themselves back into the car for one last trip, complaining about having their full tummies squashed by sitters-on, and implying that the sitters-on had become a stone or two heavier in the last hour. Just as Gerry turned the key in the ignition, there was a rap at his window. Nuala looked to see who it was, and said something that sounded suspiciously like a very rude word.

'Afternoon, Guard,' said Gerry, rolling down the window and looking the picture of nonchalance.

The stout and red-faced member of the Garda Síochána outside the car took a considering look at the girls piled two deep in the back seat, plus two more in the boot. He seemed to decide something and then change his mind.

'Your tax disc is out of date,' he said importantly.

'Oh, so it is, Guard, nicely spotted there.' Gerry was laying it on a little thick, Lilac thought, as she tried to melt into the seat beneath her and felt herself going bright red again, even though they were all very much in this together and it wasn't her fault at all. 'I think I have the new one right here in the glove compartment. Nuala, can you check, my love?'

Nuala leaned forward and produced the new, purple, tax disc, still in its little clear-plastic-on-one-side envelope. She handed it to Gerry without looking at the policeman at all. The girls barely breathed. Someone farted.

Gerry slipped the old brown disc out of its place on the windscreen and slotted the new one in.

'There we go, Guard, good as new. Thanks for the reminder.'

'You've not far to go now, have you.' It was more a statement than a question.

'Just up the road to drop these lovely ladies home to their abodes,' Gerry said, as if having eight people in a smallish car was perfectly reasonable.

'Grand so.' The guard tapped the top of the car in dismissal and took a step back. Gerry rolled up the window and the car coasted off, smooth as butter.

CHAPTER 26

Margery Dearest,

Guess who's working at the library now? Danny, Caroline's old boyfriend! He was there on Monday after school when I brought back my books. I wasn't certain it was him because I'd only seen him that one time you pointed him out to me at the shopping centre, but then one of the other librarians came to talk to him about putting things on the shelf in the wrong order and he called him Danny, so it must be him. He looks much nicer than he used to. He doesn't have that little moustache thing any more. And he helped me find a book. I didn't say anything about knowing you and Caroline, of course, because I don't talk to people about other people any more. Every time I do that I just get people into trouble. 'People' being mostly me.

Naomi got on so well with Ev at my party that I heard them planning to see each other some time when it's not even my next birthday party. I suppose I should be insulted that maybe they don't want me to be there too, but I'm happy that they each made a friend. Sometimes I feel like Naomi is too, sort of, teenagery for me, even though she's only been eleven since December. Though Ev looks more teenagery than she sounds when you get talking to her.

I suppose nobody's actually normal. Normal is just what I call the people who are most like me. You, for instance. You're fairly normal. I think. Please still be normal when you come back from Canada.

Xs and Os

Lilac

Lilac had already written Margery a big long letter about the party. This was the second one in two days, because she had to tell Margery about seeing Danny before she forgot.

'Are we invited to your wedding, Miss Grey?' Theresa Quirke asked on Wednesday when she was meant to be looking over her spelling words. It sounded pretty brazen, just out in the open like that, but it had been a topic of conversation among the class for a good while now and it was a relief to hear Theresa getting straight to the point. Everyone held their breath.

Miss Grey looked up slowly. The question didn't seem to be a surprise to her. 'No, I'm afraid you're not, girls.'

'But you see us every day. We're like the people in your office. If you had an office. You'd invite the people you work with to your wedding, wouldn't you?'

'No. No, I don't really see it like that, Theresa. You're more like my customers. If I had a shop, I couldn't invite all the people who came in every day to my wedding. I'd probably just invite the other people who worked behind the counter with me.'

The class felt collectively a little insulted. They saw themselves as much more important to Miss Grey's life than people coming and going in a shop, spending twenty pence on a packet of crisps or buying a newspaper. Katie Byrne piped up.

'I think our parents are your customers. They're the ones who want you to teach us. We're . . . we're . . .'

'We're the milk and the bread in the shop, then,' said Lilac, taking the thought to its logical conclusion. 'We're here all the time but we're just in the middle. We don't actually matter.'

This was not the direction Miss Grey had planned the conversation taking when she predicted that the question of being invited might come up. She scrambled to reassure everyone. 'No, no, you're not milk and bread. You're people.'

'It's a metaphor, Miss Grey,' Lilac reminded her. They all knew about metaphors.

'Yes, of course it is. I mean, you're much more important to me than commodities in a shop. You're not things. You're . . . vessels for me to fill up with knowledge.'

She smiled as she said it, knowing they'd find that hilarious.

'Vessels are things. Are we like Tupperware?' Katie Byrne decided to take the conversation in a new direction.

'I keep losing my lid!' Adele Duffy wailed, flailing her arms wildly. She was into method acting this week.

'My mam went to a Tupperware party once. Only then it turned out to be a lingerie party instead and she was morto,' said Laura Devine, always happy to pick up a tangent and run with it.

'Girls. I can't invite you to the wedding because you saw how many guests we have already. There isn't space. And we're not inviting children, mostly, except close family.'

Being called children was almost worse than being bread or milk or Tupperware. Everyone glowered at Miss Grey. She relented a little, though she knew she shouldn't.

'Well. I suppose I can tell you that the parish church is a public place, of course, where anyone can go, if they're respectful and quiet and polite, even if there's a ceremony going on. Now. That's all I'm saying on the subject.'

'Right. So,' Theresa Quirke began. A council of war had been called in the playground at lunchtime. Except not actually war, as Agatha pointed out, because what was less warlike than a wedding? Unless it was a really bad wedding, she supposed.

'We know the wedding is on the twenty-seventh of June, and weddings are always at three o'clock. And we can go to the church even if we're not actually invited. That's what she told us. What are we going to do?'

'We're going to . . . go to the church?' hazarded Angela Delaney.

'Yes, but what else? Will we take up a collection for a big present and give it to her there? Or write a song and sing it to her?'

'Just no interpretative dances, please,' said Lilac, and the others who had been in that group nodded vigorously in agreement.

'It could be a wedding that was arranged between the son and daughter of two warring tribes, as a truce,' Agatha said suddenly. Then she realised she'd spoken out loud by mistake. 'Sorry. That was a conversation I was having in my head. Never mind.'

Theresa shook her head over Agatha's dottiness. 'Balloons? Giant teddy? A carriage clock? What do people get for wedding presents?'

'My parents got five toasters and gave the extra four away to other people for their weddings,' Adele offered.

'My parents got a pair of giant wooden candlesticks that are totally useless,' said Lilac. 'But we can't afford to buy her a toaster or a clock, and anyway, it should be something special from us, not the sort of thing she'd get from boring other people.'

'We could make a giant card and all write poems in it. She would treasure it forever,' suggested Agatha, who liked writing poems.

'OK, let's make a list and vote on it,' said Theresa in a rounding-up way. She was really quite organized. 'I have a notebook here. Tell me all the ideas one by one.'

They listed everything they'd come up with and a few more besides – a new cardigan, two tickets to Funderland, a pledge from next year's class to always do their homework, a new blackboard duster. Then Theresa read them out one by one and everyone voted on their favourite. That narrowed it down to about ten options, because most people just voted for their own suggestion.

'This isn't working,' said Lilac impatiently. 'I think we need to actually talk about what's a sensible idea and what's not going to work. And how much money we can afford between us. That way we'll know if we can buy something or if we need to do something free.'

'We could always do both,' said Jenny O optimistically. 'Buy her something and do something as well.'

'Could everyone give 50p by two weeks from now?' Theresa asked. Everyone paused to consider their pocket money, their savings, and the other very important allocations for their precious income: buying penny sweets, paying library fines, saving for a Walkman . . . .'Maybe' was the consensus.

'Don't just ask your parents for money. This is from us. It's special. To show her that we're not just Tupperware.'

'She knows we're not.'

'You know what I mean.'

'Fine. So if we had 50p from most people, we'd have ten pounds to spend. What could we get with that?'

'Nice cardigans are expensive. We couldn't just get one from Dunnes.'

'Funderland is really good, but then you've gone and it's over.'

'And some people throw up after the rides.'

'If we gave her a blackboard duster she'd use it every day so she'd never forget us. And we could get a little plaque engraved and stick it on saying it was from us.'

'How much do dusters cost?'

'I dunno but probably not much. The plaque engraving might cost a bit.'

'And then we could buy one of those giant cards with a picture of a teddy holding flowers on it and all sign it.'

'And that way people who wanted to write a poem could write a poem.'

'And it would be almost like giving her a giant teddy and flowers as well.'

The enthusiasm was catching. People were tripping over their words with excitement about what a perfect present it would be. It was agreed that Theresa would collect the money and Lilac would find out about board dusters and engraving, and that they would all meet again for a progress update on Monday.

CHAPTER 27

'Dad, do you know how to engrave a plaque?'

'No, indeed 'n' I don't.'

'Ah Dad, I bet you do. You could do that lovely fancy writing like you do on birthday cards; all you have to do is scratch it on some metal.'

'No, Lilac, you need to go to a professional for that.'

'Well, where do I find a professional, then?'

'Look them up in the phone book. The golden pages. Or I think Byrne's Hardware might have something; maybe you should ask your man in the shop.'

Lilac hitched Guzzler to his lead and went for a walk down the town, to the hardware shop at the bottom of the hill. It took a bit of explaining to Mr Byrne behind the counter to get across what they were thinking of doing, because apparently attaching an engraved plaque to a blackboard duster was not an everyday task, but once he figured out what she meant, he was very helpful.

'Now, missy, this is what you can take back to your classmates. Are ya listening to me?'

'Yes.' Lilac's eyes got big and round with concentration, and she tried not to blink.

'You need to work out exactly the words you want to put on it, because you've only a small bit of space there to work with, right?'

'Right.'

'And you'll have to buy the duster in somewhere like Eason's because I don't stock those myself. But I can do the rest for you if you bring it in to me.'

'Right.'

'And I'll need to have it at least a week in advance.'

'Yes.'

'And it'll cost four pounds seventy-five for the plaque and the engraving and attaching it. I'm giving you a special bargain now, because you're a loyal customer. You and your daddy, that is.'

Mr Byrne winked at her, because Lilac's dad bought quite a lot of things there to paint with, even though it was a hardware shop and he was a picture painter, not a house painter. They had a little art-supply section that seemed to be getting bigger, maybe mostly thanks to Gerry. At least, that's what Lilac hoped the wink was about, because she'd never bought anything in there herself before.

Dear Lilac

You are in BIG TROUBLE. At least, you would be if things hadn't worked out OK but I think you're off the hook for now.

I'm still pretty annoyed with you though because you couldn't have known it would work out OK and if it hadn't I would have been in ENORMOUS TROUBLE with Caroline and that's not the sort of trouble you should wish upon your worst enemy let alone someone you say is your best friend.

Yours sincerely,

Margery

Lilac had no idea what this was about. What could she possibly have done that would get Margery in trouble with Caroline? They were on different continents; you'd think that would be actually totally impossible. There had been that time last year when something Margery said in a letter got back to the girls in her class and was taken up in entirely the wrong way, but that was a one-off event. And Lilac was very careful with what she said to Jeannie about Caroline now that she knew they knew each other.

There was something niggling at the back of her mind, though. She couldn't quite get it to come all the way to the front and show itself. Maybe she'd wait to write back asking Margery what she was on about until Lilac had figured out what it was that she wasn't remembering . . .

CHAPTER 28

'Lilac! Granny's on the phone! Do you want to come and say hi?'

Lilac jumped up from her Sunday evening Irish-homework extravaganza and clattered down the stairs and into the kitchen. She particularly wanted to talk to Granny: in all the excitement of the tennis club musical and the Confirmation and the birthday while Granny was visiting, she never had got around to asking for detective-like help with finding Michael's missing things. She took the phone from Nuala's hand and shooed her out of the room.

'Hi Granny! How are you?'

'Lilac, darling, I'm fine, thank you. And how's yourself? You'd a lovely party, I hear.'

'It was really nice. Though I think Dad nearly got arrested at the end of it.'

'Oh he did, did he? Up to no good again, that son-in-law of mine, the miscreant.' Lilac knew Granny was a big fan of Gerry, so she was just joking.

'Granny, are you really a secret agent? Or a spy?

Because I forgot to ask you about this when you were here, but my friend Michael and I were wondering if you could solve the mystery of his missing stuff. Michael thinks they were burgled, and you were here when Mum was talking about people in the tennis club having break-ins, remember? Do you have any leads? Or maybe do you have any spying equipment you could lend me?'

The nice thing about Granny was that she never brushed off Lilac's concerns as childish nonsense. She rose to the occasion with a perfectly serious response. 'Now, child,' she said warningly. 'The only spying equipment I have is my own two eyes, and you have a perfectly good pair of those yourself. And you're the one who's in the right place to look for leads.'

'But I was thinking you might have some connections. You could help me tap some phones or something.'

'Phone tapping indeed. As if I'd know anything about that.' Granny was just being cagey, Lilac could tell. 'And whose phone would you be tapping, if you don't have any leads yet?'

'I suppose that's true. I need to get the leads first. Well, how would you start if it was your case, Granny?'

'I'd keep my eyes open. And talk to people, but mostly listen to what they have to say. And I'd remember that appearances can be deceptive.'

'That's good advice.' Lilac nodded seriously. 'See, I knew you were a secret agent.'

'Ah, get on with you now, child.' Lilac could hear the smile in Granny's voice and she knew her eyes were crinkled with amusement. Lilac was pretty sure that was because she was proud of her clever granddaughter who had figured out her secret.

'I won't tell a soul, I promise. Oh, except Michael, because I already did. But sure, you're retired now.'

'Give the phone back to your mum for a minute, and you go on back to your homework. It was lovely to talk to you.'

'You too, Granny. Bye.' Lilac put her hand over the mouthpiece and shouted in the direction of the kitchen door. 'Muuuuum! Granny wants you back!' Then she handed over the phone and went back upstairs, to make a list. Irish spellings could wait.

'Um, hi. Can Michael come out? Just for a minute.'

Michael had been so helpful the last time Lilac made a list – because after all, the whole Shrove/Ursula debacle hadn't been *his* fault – that she thought she'd ask him for help again. And because it was his mystery, after all. And also because she felt this might help rescue their friendship, since things weren't quite back to normal after Jeannie hearing the Hyacinth story. Hyacinth himself – that is, David – answered the door, and Lilac could barely look him in the eye, but she managed to mumble out a sentence and he disappeared soon enough. She wasn't even sure David knew who she was.

'Mary!' he shouted as he turned away from the door. 'Lilac's here looking for you!'

Oh. He did know, then. Michael came out, bright red, and shut the door behind him. 'You didn't hear David say that, right?'

'Say what? Nope, he didn't say a thing.' Lilac wasn't born yesterday. She was savvy to the ways of brothers. At least savvy enough to pretend she hadn't heard what David called him.

They wandered towards the park at the end of the road, and she explained about her conversation with Granny, and Granny's good advice. 'She didn't exactly say it, but I'm pretty sure she meant that if we found some suspects she could probably arrange a phone tap. All those hints about listening to people. I got her drift.'

'What's a phone tap?'

'You know, when they put a wire into someone's phone and connect it to a tape recorder so that you can listen to what they're saying and catch them in the act. It was in the news a while ago.'

'But isn't that illegal? Isn't that what the news was about?'

'Oh no, not if you do it right.'

'Oh. OK.'

'So we need to figure out our suspects. And maybe interview the people who were burgled. Or people who might be burgled. So we can detect a pattern. Who do you think we should talk to first?'

'But don't you think the Gardaí have done all that? What could we find out that they couldn't?'

'Haven't you read any Enid Blyton at all? Don't you know that kids find out things that adults don't, because nobody thinks that kids are paying attention, so they let their guard down and say things they shouldn't? And then it turns out that kids pay more attention than anyone else.' Lilac knew how these things worked. At least in fiction.

'I don't. Dad always says I don't notice anything.'

'My dad says that too. I think it's just a Dad thing to say.

I don't think it means anything.'

They had reached the park now. Lilac automatically sat in the swing and gave herself a little push with her legs to get going. Michael sat on the end of the slide, avoiding the puddle that was nearly always there, thinking hard. Lilac racked her brain to come up with some possible suspects. Her notebook was still in her hand, doubled around the chain of the swing, with a pencil pushed into its spiralled wire spine.

'But I don't know anyone who could be a burglar,' Michael complained. 'All the people I know are friends of my parents, or my teachers, and they all have other jobs. They wouldn't have time to be going to people's houses in the middle of the night and nicking their stuff. Someone would notice.'

'OK.' Lilac felt she had to be extra nice to him, since she was rescuing their friendship, so she gave him an easier task. 'How about thinking about anything suspicious you've seen lately. Something that doesn't fit in. Someone who looked odd. Anything?'

'Something suspicious? Well, all our stuff going missing, that was pretty suspicious.' Michael sounded grumpy.

'Come on, you're not trying. I'm thinking too, honestly.' She got off the swing and sat on the edge of the sandpit, opening her notebook and extracting the pencil, ready to write. 'OK, tell me about what happened, exactly. Which thing disappeared first?'

'We don't know, really. The first thing someone noticed was when David couldn't find those earrings he'd bought for Jeannie. Except he wouldn't tell us for ages what it was he was missing because he didn't want to admit he had a girlfriend, so he just went stomping around giving out that he'd lost something.'

'And then?'

'And then I wanted to listen to my Walkman and I couldn't find my headphones.'

'But are you sure they're not just lost?'

'I thought they must be but I've looked everywhere. And also I know where I left them because I'm really careful with them, since I bought them with my own money from my birthday, and they weren't there.'

'And Jimmy couldn't have taken them?'

'I asked him. I held him upside down and tickled him and he still didn't squeal. I mean, squeal in the sense of telling the truth, the way gangsters say it. He did *actually* squeal, because he loves being tickled. Also, I looked in all his hiding places.'

'And what was the third thing?'

'My dad's silver heirloom, remember? He keeps stuff in it, he said, but he wouldn't say what. And he said it was in a drawer, it wasn't out. I don't really know what it looks like, I don't remember seeing it before.'

'Did you see any signs of a break-in?'

'No, not exactly. But it might have happened a while earlier and we didn't think to notice anything. They must be sneak thieves. Cat burglars.'

Lilac nodded as she took notes. Cat burglars sounded good. Dressed all in black, tiptoeing from room to room, wearing gloves to avoid leaving fingerprints. 'Well, you'll have to interview the others and see if they noticed anything. Anything at all.'

'Noticed anything when? Ever? How do I ask them

that?'

'No, not *ever*. In the time when things went missing. I mean . . .' Lilac felt this was much harder than it should be. Surely real detectives didn't have this much trouble just figuring out what it was they were looking for. 'I'll ask my mum about the people from the tennis club who had break-ins. Maybe we can find a pattern in the things they do that will tell us more about who it could be.'

It was starting to get dark. 'I still have homework to finish,' Michael said. 'I'd better go in. Come on, Jimmy!'

Lilac was startled to see that Jimmy had been on the other side of the trees the whole time, quietly eavesdropping while he pulled the wings off flies, or whatever it was he did. For once, he decided to come in when he was called, and he loped back up the road after Michael and Lilac, slow-motion running as if he was the Six Million Dollar Man, executing a quick roll along the pavement from time to time as he went.

CHAPTER 29

The next morning, as Lilac lay in bed in that lovely state between sleeping and waking that happens on May mornings when the sunlight rouses you before you need to get up, a thought came to her. A thought that was such genius she was almost startled by it.

The man in the tweed cap! The man she'd seen twice the day she bought her Easter egg, and then again outside Ev's house the day of her party! The man who didn't mind being rained on. That was strange, and so was the fact that he wore a much older man's cap, and the way Guzzler hadn't growled at him. All those things were strange, and strange was exactly what she was on the lookout for.

He was casing the joints! He was looking at all the houses planning to burgle them. He was disguised (badly) as an older man so that nobody would suspect that he was actually light-footed and lithe and well able to sneak around cat-burgling. He kept dog treats in his pockets to make friends with guard dogs. They might even be drugged! Poor Guzzler had had a narrow escape.

She leapt out of bed and scribbled a new heading in her notebook:

SUSPECTS (To Investigate)

Then she wrote underneath it: '1. Man in Cap.' She chewed her pen for a few minutes in case any more bursts of genius would elicit more names for the list, but the more she thought about it, the more she was convinced that this was a short list pointing directly to the culprit. It had to be the man in the cap.

She couldn't wait to tell Michael and see if he'd noticed the man anywhere, as she was sure he would have once she jogged his memory, but it was a school morning and Michael left the house early on weekdays. So she brought her notebook downstairs to put in her schoolbag, because it also contained the list of things Mr Byrne had told her to tell the girls about the engraving. Then she poured herself an enormous bowl of Rice Krispies and settled down to finish her book over breakfast in a quiet kitchen.

A little while later, getting dressed, Lilac looked again at Margery's puzzling letter and scribbled a quick response.

Dear Margery,

I don't know what you're talking about. I honestly truely don't have a clue. I'm glad you say things worked out OK and I'm sorry if I accidentally did something terrible. But please don't accuse me of things when I didn't do things and I don't

even know what they are. I don't appreciate that. A little
faith in me would be nice.
  Your friend,
  Lilac

Halfway through apologising for this thing she had
apparently done, Lilac got miffed with Margery for
assuming the worst without even checking, so the letter
ended more quickly than she had intended. But really,
what sort of uncivilised country was this if you couldn't just
live your life without being accused of doing something
terrible to someone who was living an ocean away, she
asked herself, certain that this time the high moral ground
was right there under her feet.

She didn't put the letter in an envelope, though. She left
it on her desk in case she might think of something more to
say later. Or, she supposed, in case she might feel more
charitable towards Margery after an interlude. Because it
was a pretty snotty letter, really.

When she got home from school Lilac found another letter
from Margery waiting for her. This one was fatter than the
last.

Dear Lilac,
  Sorry sorry sorry. At least, I think sorry. It's just
possible that maybe you don't know what my last letter
was talking about. It's just possible that you didn't on

purpose give Danny my photo of me and Caroline when we were small and tell him that's who it was. Though I can't imagine how else he could have come across it. And you said you saw him at the library.

But I suppose I didn't explain what happened and I probably should have done, whether you meant it to turn out well or not. Mum says I should give you the benefit of the doubt and think that even if you did it on purpose, it was because you saw that Danny is nicer now and you thought it might make him see a nicer side of Caroline. The girl behind the mask, maybe. (Mask of caked-on foundation and blue eyeshadow, more like.) He did sound nice in his letter. Caroline even let me read it.

So this is what happened. Danny SOMEHOW got hold of that photo I sent you that you said you'd treasure forever. And he could tell exactly who it was because I'd written it on the back. And HE SAYS he decided it was a message from Fate telling him to write to Caroline and send it back to her in case she'd accidentally lost it. So he did, and he was all lovey dovey (puke) and explained why he hadn't written at all when we went away first and he said 'You are my density' which is a joke from Back to the Future which they saw together in the cinema. And she got all sniffly at the breakfast table reading the letter. And I think she really loves him.

So she wrote back and now they're back together, except Long Distance, because you can't be actually together when you're 5000 miles apart. He even rang her on Saturday night and they spent ten minutes on the phone and he gave his mum a tenner for the phone bill. He must be a reformed character to do that. And she's happy because all her plans and hopes and dreams and wishes have come true. At least her most recent ones where she wanted to get back together with him. Not the ones she had last month when she was really upset at Jean-Claude for dumping her. (She wasn't the one who broke it off after all.)

So it's all OK whether you meant it to happen or not. And I don't even know if I hope you did or you didn't because I do still feel a bit like you broke my trust either way. But sorry, I suppose, for my last letter, because it might have been jumping to conclusions a bit.

Luv,

Margery

This was all quite a surprise to Lilac. Of course she hadn't given Danny the photo, but she realised that the niggly feeling she had was because she'd left her bookmark in the book she brought back to the library. And the bookmark was the photo. It must have fallen out when Danny checked it back in or put it back on the shelf or something. So it was her fault, but not on purpose. She ripped up her snotty letter to Margery and started a nicer one instead.

CHAPTER 30

Lilac's only homework was to do something nice for someone else and then write about it. Miss Grey wasn't really putting much effort into homework requirements these days, what with 'her upcoming nuptials', as Sister Joseph had put it when she took them for a choir practice in the middle of the day. They didn't usually have choir on Mondays, but Miss Grey had had to rush out to the florist to sort out some terrible mistake involving petunias, so Sister Joseph had stepped in.

Theresa Quirke took the opportunity to ask as much as she could about Miss Grey's wedding plans. All the teachers sat around a big table every lunchtime chatting about Miss Grey's wedding while they ate their sandwiches – at least, that was what Lilac and the others assumed – so Sister Joseph should know all about it.

'Sister, do you know what colours Miss Grey is having?'

'Colours? Colours for what, child?'

'For her wedding, Sister. Like, will her bridesmaids be peach or pink? Will her flowers be red roses or carnations?

Will there be balloons or ribbons for decorations? Where are they going on their honeymoon?' Theresa's cousin had just got married, so Theresa was familiar with the important decisions that had to be made by every bride. 'Does her dress have big puff sleeves and a long train and a huge veil?'

That one was a bit of a foregone conclusion, though. The girls knew that every beautiful wedding dress had big puff sleeves and a long train and a huge veil. And Miss Grey had lovely taste, so hers surely would too.

But Sister Joseph was cagey. Either she wasn't in Miss Grey's confidence, or she wasn't telling. 'Theresa, child, weddings are hardly my area of expertise. You can direct your attention to the music in front of you. That, I do know something about – and you certainly don't,' said the nun pointedly.

'She's just jealous,' Jenny O whispered to Lilac, elbowing her in the ribs. 'She doesn't ever get to plan a wedding. Bet she didn't think of that when she decided to be a nun.'

That afternoon Lilac decided she'd probably end up doing something nice for homework without even trying. She could just think later what it had been and write it down. She went to call on Michael to tell him about her burglary-related brainwave.

'Michael's doing his homework,' his mother said when she opened the front door. 'At least, I think he is. Michael!' She shouted up the stairs, but Michael emerged from the kitchen behind her, cramming one piece of buttered toast into his mouth and holding a second in his hand. 'Oh, there you are. Don't you have homework?'

'Not really. We have to write about a book we read this year, and I already did that. So I can just copy it out again. He won't notice. He's not paying much attention to us any more. It's too close to summer holidays, I think.'

'Oh, all right then, out you go.' Michael's mother always seemed slightly harried, worn down by years of mothering boys and caring for a crotchety mother-in-law at the same time. She closed the door behind them. Lilac and Michael wandered in the direction of the playground, since that seemed to be their habit now. It was starting to rain, but only lightly. If they stayed under the trees they'd hardly notice anything.

'My teacher's like that too these days. But she's getting married. Otherwise she'd still care about what we were learning, I'm sure,' said Lilac.

'Mr O'Grady doesn't have an excuse. At least, not one he's told us about. He's just bored with teaching, I think. He's been at the school for years. He keeps calling me David because he was David's teacher too. And then he's surprised when I'm no good at Irish, because David was.'

Lilac imagined an irritable old man, near retirement age, in a tweedy jacket with leather patches on the elbows. She pitied Michael, not having a nice young teacher like Miss Grey. At least when Miss Grey stared into space and forgot what she was saying to them, they knew it was because she was so much in love with her fiancé that she couldn't keep her mind on her job. It was terribly romantic, so the girls went easy on her.

'Anyway.' Lilac brought her mind back to the matter at

hand. 'I thought of a suspect. For the burglaries.'

'Did you? Who?'

'The man in the cap.'

'The man in the cap. Right. What man is that?'

'OK, listen and tell me if this sounds familiar. I bet you've seen him hanging around too. He's young but he wears a grey tweed cap as if he's an auld fella. He smiles at everyone in this weird way as if he knows them and they already like him, even if they've never met him before. He talks too much. He wants to know everyone's name. I've seen him on our road, and down at the shops, and even at my friend Ev's house. And – this is the most suspicious thing – when it started pouring rain he didn't even look like he cared if he got wet.'

Michael nodded at each thing Lilac said, and furrowed his brow, and looked like he was concentrating as hard as he possibly could, but finally he shook his head.

'Nope. No, I don't think I've seen him anywhere.' Lilac was downcast. 'But,' Michael continued, 'it sounds good. I mean, that all sounds pretty suspicious. Sort of. As if he could be looking for houses to break into and talking to people to find out if they're rich and where they live.'

'Exactly. That's what I thought. So now we just have to see him again and follow him to his lair. I mean, his hideout. And then we can look in the window and see all the stuff he's stolen stashed there, and then we can call the police and have him arrested and get all the stuff back.' Lilac's plan spread out before her like an unfolded road map. One thing led straight to the next.

'Or we could just ask someone who he is.' Michael wasn't so sure that was how it would go. But then, he hadn't seen the man. He couldn't understand just how obviously he was the culprit.

'But who would know? He's probably operating under a false name. A whatchamacallit – an alias.' Lilac knew how these shady types operated. She'd been practising for this since the day she first opened a *Secret Seven*.

'Right. If he *is* the burglar.'

'I bet he is. He has to be.'

There was a pause.

'What was the book you wrote about?' Lilac wanted to know.

'Well, it's not exactly a book. But it was very educational. An *Asterix* comic. A big long one about the Roman Empire. I wrote a book review on it last year, but I can just copy it out again and fix the spellings and Mr O'Grady won't know.'

'That sounds interesting.' Lilac was mostly just being polite. She had no idea what an *Asterix* comic would be like.

'I can lend it to you if you want. It's really funny.'

'OK, thanks.' A comic wouldn't take long to read, though she didn't see how Michael could get away with calling it a book. But that's what she got for being polite. Maybe this could count as the nice thing she'd done today, and she could write about it for *her* homework. Two birds, one stone.

CHAPTER 31

A few days later, Lilac rode her new bike back down to Byrne's Hardware to order the engraving for Miss Grey's present. She brought with her a blackboard duster, which Aisling Bond's mum had bought in Woolworth's (with money from the class, of course), and a piece of paper with the wording exactly as they wanted it, and a purse full of 50p pieces. The duster fit perfectly in a hand, a pleasantly solid oblong of smooth varnished yellow wood on top, with grooves on either side to grip it by. Underneath, it had the softest, blackest, most velvety fluff she had ever seen on such an item – because of course it was brand new and had never yet encountered chalk dust.

Lilac felt a little sorry for it, because once it started its job in a classroom, it would never again look so clean and perfect. On the other hand, she thought, this was what its whole existence so far had led up to; this was what it had trained for, all those months at duster academy, doing sit-ups and running laps and whatever exercises dusters had to do to prepare for a lifetime of cleaning blackboards.

Maybe it was looking forward to finally getting to grips with some real classroom chalk. And it would be an extra special duster too, treasured forever by Miss Grey, because it would remind her of the wonderful class who gave it to her, and of the year she got married. When she was old and wizened and still teaching fifth class, the girls would look with wonder at the lovely engraving and marvel at what a perfect present that perfect class had given their Miss Grey.

Of course, she'd be Mrs someone by then. Lilac didn't know what Miss Grey's new name would be. They hadn't asked her. Obviously, she was marrying some man or other, who was presumably tall and dark and handsome; but the class was much more interested in the details of dresses and bridesmaids and decorations than in who it might be that was winning the hand of their fair maiden.

All this musing got Lilac as far as Mr Byrne's door before she had even begun to collect her thoughts about what she would say. He was behind his cash register at the front of the shop as usual, looking red-faced and cheerful and ready to wink at her and say something confusing, no doubt. Lilac liked Mr Byrne, but sometimes he made her a little uncomfortable. She liked to have her words prepared before she got there, so he didn't fluster her into forgetting what she meant to say.

'Aha, young lady. And what can I do you for?' He winked, right on cue.

'Hello, Mr Byrne.' She tried her best to sound businesslike, to discourage the winking. 'I have the duster here and we've written down the words for the engraving. And I have the money to pay you in advance because everyone brought in their 50p's already.'

'Indeed you do, I see that, a lovely duster you've got there, and this . . .' He fumbled for his glasses, didn't find them, and stretched out his hand to read the torn-out notebook page at arm's length '. . . right, then. Are you sure that's what you want to say?'

'Yes, definitely. It's sort of a secret code, you see.'

'Grand so, I'll take it to my grave, not a word.' Another wink.

'Well, I mean, it won't be secret once we give it to her. But it's sort of a private joke.'

'I won't ask.' He tapped the side of his nose and nodded slowly.

'And here's the money.' Lilac up-ended her open purse on the counter. The coins didn't all roll away because almost all of them were fifty pence pieces with seven flat sides each. She counted them up one more time, so that he could see they were all there, and gave him all nine, plus a shiny new 20p coin with a horse on it and one 5p-that-used-to-be-a-shilling.

'Four pounds seventy-five, as we said, all in order,' Mr Byrne agreed, shunting them into his cash register and pushing the drawer closed with a satisfying ding. He put an elastic band around the duster and pushed the folded-up piece of paper under it to keep the two together, and then he put them away somewhere under the counter, onto what Lilac hoped was his 'Things To Engrave' shelf. She said thank you and turned to go, but he called her back.

'Ah, hang on there a sec while I have you, missy. I have something for your daddy – maybe you could give it to him. He asked me to take a look and see if I could get it open without damaging it any more. Nice wee piece. I've wrapped it up now, so don't go peeking. I'm sure he'll show you if he wants to. I left what was in it inside, though it won't be much use to anyone any more.' And with that he handed over a plastic bag with something in brown paper at the bottom, about the shape and size of a pack of playing cards.

'Um, OK, I'll give it to him,' said Lilac, wondering what all that was about, and left the shop, happy to escape without any more winks.

When Lilac got home, Gerry was washing brushes at the kitchen sink. She took him to task. 'You know Mum hates you doing that there. You get paint on the dishes and then we eat the paint and it's bad for us and it'll probably kill us. She says.'

'Ah now, what the eye doesn't see, the heart doesn't grieve after,' said her father in an old-man voice. 'Don't say a word. My sink in the studio's so full of everything else that there's no room to wash a quick brush or two.'

'Mr Byrne gave me this for you. What is it?' Lilac demanded, putting the package from the plastic bag on the table.

'Well, how would I know? I haven't looked at it yet. Open it up there, go on. My hands are wet,' he said flapping an elbow in her direction. She'd been hoping he'd say that. As she unwound the brown paper, she realised what it must be.

'It's the silver box, isn't it? The one I found on the beach? I forgot all about it.'

'Guzzler found, I thought you said. Yes, that's what it is. Did he get it to open?'

'I think he said he did.' She brought it out, still as shiny as a mirror. 'It looks even brighter than I remember. He must have polished it again.' She tried the lid, just a little. It didn't stick. 'It opens!' The corner where it had been jammed shut was a tiny bit buckled still, but Mr Byrne seemed to have done a good job and it looked almost like new. Or at least, as Lilac imagined it would have looked when it was new. Probably fifty years ago at least.

She opened it and looked at the contents. About ten cigarettes sat there, looking bent and sort of shrivelled, as if they had once been very wet and then dried out again. But then, more interestingly, she caught sight of an inscription on the inside of the lid. In curly letters that were hard to read, it said: 'To Fred with love – Avril.'

'Oh,' she said unenthusiastically, turning the box around so Gerry could see what was inside. 'But look at this!' She pointed to the words. 'Do you think Avril gave Fred the cigarettes? And he never got them? Or he didn't like smoking so he threw it away and broke up with her?' The possibilities were endless.

Lilac's imagination went into overdrive, seeing in her mind's eye a man in a bow tie and a top hat and an elegant woman in a long drapey gown with one of those old-fashioned cigarette holders between long delicate fingers ... *No, Avril, I cannot marry you after all. You won't give up that filthy habit for me, and now you want me to take it up too. The silver box is lovely, but I can't do it. My lungs won't thank you.*

Of course, they didn't know about lungs back then, or at least about what cigarettes would do to them. But he still mightn't have liked the idea of smoking. Maybe he was afraid he'd accidentally set his top hat on fire. It was so shiny, it was probably highly flammable.

Her dad brought her back to reality. 'I don't think it's originally a cigarette case, Lilac; and those smokes certainly aren't as old as the inscription. I think someone's just been using it to keep their cigarettes in – but not Fred or Avril. They probably had a long, happy life together. Let's believe they did.'

'Wait, there's a note here from Mr Byrne.' Lilac had turned the box over and found a note taped to the bottom. 'It says, "Silvermark indicates made in Birmingham, 1907." Wow! I wonder who they were. Did people wear top hats in 1907, Dad?' Lilac wanted to know if her imagination was right about one thing, at least.

'Yes, probably. Rich people.'

'Well, you'd have to be rich to buy a silver box to not keep your cigarettes in, wouldn't you?'

'I suppose you would.'

'Good.'

Gerry didn't ask why she wanted to know about top hats. He was used to Lilac's trains of thought jumping the tracks and heading down unpredictable branch lines. His brushes were clean and he headed back to his painting room, already contemplating his next strokes.

'Thanks for getting it fixed, Dad!'

'Sure. You'll have to think what to do with it now, though. Do you think someone might be looking for it?'

'Oh.' Lilac hadn't considered that before. When Guzzler dug the box up on the beach, she'd thought it came under the finders-keepers rule. But then, if it had been expensive in 1907, it was perhaps worth even more today. Avril and Fred probably hadn't just thrown it away. But wait, assuming they were grown-ups in 1907 – at least twenty, let's say – they'd be . . . 100 now, in 1987. Maybe not Avril and Fred, then – but perhaps their family members. The box could be – what was that word Michael had used? – an *air-loom*, that was it.

Even though she'd forgotten all about it for a while, now that Lilac saw the pretty little silver box again she felt very fond of it. She wanted it to be hers; but she thought about how much more special it would be if it had belonged to her grandfather or great-grandfather. If someone out there had lost it, she needed to reunite it with its family. She should bring it to the Garda station, she supposed, to see if they had a report of its being missing.

'Oh!' she said again, though nobody was left in the room to hear her. Guzzler pricked up his ears for a second, but then he went back to sleep. The burglaries! It might have been stolen by those thieves who were taking silver things. But then, how did it end up on the beach instead of in Man in Cap's hideout? Could he have dropped it as he made his getaway? Over the stones of the beach? To . . . avoid leaving footprints? That seemed like a bit of a stretch, even for Lilac's vivid imagination. No, she decided. It had no connection to the burglaries. But she should bring it to the station anyway. And then, she thought, looking on the bright side, if nobody *had* reported it missing she'd probably get to keep it after all.

'Tomorrow,' she announced for the benefit of the sleeping Guzzler. 'I'll bring it tomorrow.' She emptied the old cigarettes into the bin and brought the box up to her bedroom where she put it on her shelf for the time being, admiring the shiny silver against the dark brown wood.

CHAPTER 32

The next morning, Lilac looked at the box again and decided that she didn't need to bring it with her when she asked at the Garda station. She could just describe it to them. That way, it would stay safe on her shelf instead of risking the dangerous journey to school and back, not to mention spending all day in her schoolbag where it could easily get kicked and dented again. Her decision had nothing to do with how nice the box looked in her bedroom and how much she wanted to keep it there.

She and Agatha walked home from school through the main street and stopped in at the Garda station, which was a little way up a narrow side road near the church. As she pushed open the heavy door, she realised she'd never been in here before. They entered a small room with a bench to sit on, some posters about how to apply for a driving test, and a window with a sliding glass part so you could talk to the guard on duty. Behind the window was a larger room with messy desks and fax machines and filing cabinets, just like any other office. There was nobody in sight.

'Maybe they're all out at a bank robbery,' said Lilac to Agatha in a half-whisper.

'Or rescuing a cat from a tree,' Agatha suggested.

'Isn't that the fire brigade?'

'Maybe it is. But what else do Gardaí do? There can't be a bank robbery to foil every day. They don't come up on the news very often at all.'

'There's a bell there. Should we ring it?'

'I don't want to. Let's just wait a minute first.' They stood staring through the window waiting to see if anything would happen.

A young guard in a white shirt with the sleeves rolled up twirled through a door into the back room, humming to himself – and then checked his cha-cha-cha as he looked up and saw the two girls standing silently at the window.

'Jaysus, don't give me a heart attack like that! Why didn't you ring the bell?' he said to them, not looking embarrassed at all to have been caught dancing.

'We thought it might be noisy,' said Lilac, which was a pretty bad reason, she realised.

'That's the idea, love,' he answered, with a grin. 'When I'm in the back drinking my cuppa and practising my tango steps, I need a good loud alarm bell to get me out here.' He approached the other side of the window and straightened his tie, putting on his official face.

'Now, what can I do for you young ladies?'

Lilac took a deep breath. 'My dog found a small silver box buried on the beach and I wondered if anyone had reported it missing,' she said, suddenly feeling a little warm around the cheeks. 'And if they hadn't, is it all right if I keep it?' she added in a rush.

The guard rustled through a stack of papers and produced a form and a pen. He slid open the window and started to hand them through to her, saying, 'Just fill this out with a description and bring the box in to me. If nobody claims it in six months, you can come and get it.'

'Six months? Could I not just mind it myself at home, and then bring it in to you if someone says it's theirs? I'll give you my phone number.'

'She's very reliable,' Agatha piped up, feeling the need to provide a character reference. 'You can ask Sister Joseph.' She assumed everyone in the town would know Sister Joseph.

'And I'm sure she is if Sister Joseph says so. But that's not how it works, I'm afraid.' For all his friendliness, the guard didn't seem willing to bend on matters of protocol.

'Oh.' Lilac took the form but not the pen. 'I'll fill it in at home, then, I suppose, and bring them back together.'

'You do that. Don't forget, now, or I'll have to go and ask Sister Joseph to remind you. Safe home, now,' he finished jovially.

Lilac stuffed the form into her schoolbag and she and Agatha flustered themselves back out again, muttering thank-yous and goodbyes. Lilac frowned as the door banged behind them.

'Now I really wish I hadn't gone. I was trying to do the right thing, but if he won't even tell me whether someone's reported it missing, and if I have to bring it in and give it to them for six months . . . *six months!*'

In six months' time, Margery would be home. They'd be in sixth class. Miss Grey would be married and they'd have a different teacher. It was too far away to even imagine.

Lilac didn't exactly plan to never hand in the box, but she did take comfort in the fact that there was a lot of stuff in her schoolbag just now and the form might possibly get misplaced at some point before she remembered to take it out and fill it in.

'I don't think he really knows Sister Joseph, do you?' she said.

'Probably not.' Agatha was good at saying what Lilac wanted to hear, even if it wasn't always strictly the truth. She fished around in her uniform pocket and extracted a few coins. 'I have 17p. Let's go into the newsagent's and buy one of each kind of penny sweet.'

CHAPTER 33

Thunk. Thunk. Thunk. THWAP.

Lilac had been ignoring the bumping noises she was hearing through her bedroom wall while she wrote to Margery, but now they were getting louder. She looked out her window to see if she could spot what was making them.

She heard a sort of strangled whisper-shout: 'Lilac!'

She looked down to see Michael in her back garden, holding a tennis ball.

'What are you doing? Why isn't Guzzler barking at you?'

'He knows me – why would he bark? I was trying to get your attention without your mum seeing me. I didn't want to call to the door.'

'But my mum is probably looking out the kitchen window at you wondering what you're doing.'

Michael focused on the kitchen window in front of him rather than Lilac's window above him. He waved sheepishly.

'Oh. She is.'

'I'll come down, wait a minute.'

Lilac ran downstairs and out the back door from the kitchen. 'Tell Michael to come in and have a drink of orange,' her mother said as she passed.

'Mum says come in and have some orange. Actually, I think we have lemon barley water if you like that.'

'No, that's the whole point.' Michael was still whispering like someone in a bad spy film. 'We have to go somewhere else.' He took her arm and tried to pull her back around to the front of the house.

'I've no shoes on, wait. Will you not just come in? We've biccies too. Though not chocolate ones.'

He shook his head. It must be serious if he was turning down a biscuit, she thought.

'OK, hang on a tick.' She ran inside, grabbed her runners from the bottom of the stairs where she'd abandoned them the day before, hopped on one foot and then the other to get back to the kitchen while putting them on, and went back outside. The laces flapped around her feet, but this was obviously a no-time-for-bunny-ears emergency.

'We need to go where nobody will hear us,' Michael said, leading the way to the street. 'Your mum already knows I'm talking to you and that's a bad thing because she's bound to work it out and then you'll be in even more trouble.'

'I'm not *in* trouble. Am I?'

'That's what I'm talking about. You are, but you don't know it. Are you smoking?'

Lilac was taken aback. 'Am I smoking? Like, cigarettes? Of course not. I'm not . . . *Maura Rooney.*' She put all the incredulity she could muster into the name, but it was lost on Michael, who didn't know that Maura was the most rebellious of the rebels in fifth class.

'Well your mum thinks you are. My mum invited her in for a cup of tea yesterday after lunch and David heard them talking about it, because Mum forgot he was in his room. He'd come straight home from the orthodontist instead of going back to school. He has train tracks now. He's pretty depressed about it.'

'Ugh, poor David. Metal-mouth.' Lilac grimaced in sympathy before coming back to what he had said first. 'Wait – what? But why does my mum think I'm smoking?'

'Because she found a load of cigarettes in the bin in your house.' He thought for a second. 'Though on the other hand, why would you throw them away if you were going to smoke them?'

Lilac's frown disappeared. 'Ohhhh. Oh, that's OK. It's fine. They weren't mine. I threw them away, but they weren't mine.'

'Then whose were they? Your dad doesn't smoke, I know, because he gave me a big lecture about it one time.'

'No, no, Dad was with me when I found them.' She explained about finding the box and getting it fixed. 'When we opened it there were cigarettes inside. But they were ruined – and anyway, yuck, cigarettes – so we threw them away. I still have the box.'

She was about to tell him about the engraving, and the sad story of how she would have to bring it to the Garda station because she'd made the fatal mistake of enquiring about it there, but he interrupted her.

'Little silver box? Like my dad's heirloom?'

'Was that a box? You never said. *Like* that, maybe. But *not* that, obviously.'

'How do you know not that? What does it look like, exactly?'

'It can't be *that*, because yours was stolen, not lost on the beach. Cap Man probably has yours at his hideout, where we'll find it just as soon as we figure out who he is and follow him back there and expose his dirty dealings. It's silver and Mr Byrne said it was made in Birmingham in 1907. It has little swirly designs around the edges, and it's about this big.' She made appropriately sized box shapes with her fingers and thumbs. 'And it was from Avril to Fred. There's an engraving. I love it.'

'Nana-nana-nana-nana Cap Maaaan,' Michael sang under his breath to the *Batman* tune. 'How are we going to figure out who he is, though? It does sounds a bit like ours, as far as I remember it. Maybe all silver boxes look like that, though.'

'Did you ask your family if they'd seen him? Or met him? I saw him in lots of places – other people must have too.'

'I can ask them tonight.'

'Right. I will too. I suppose I'd better go and tell Mum I'm not giving myself lung cancer. Next time you want me, just ring the doorbell instead of playing tennis against my back wall.'

'I wasn't playing tennis, I was gently tossing the ball at your window. Because there wasn't any gravel.'

'That's even worse. Don't break my window to get my attention.'

'People always throw gravel at windows in books. It doesn't break them.'

'But with my luck, it would.'

'I suppose.'

'Race you to my gate.'

'Go!'

Lilac would have won, but she tripped over her laces and skinned her knee instead. Michael made sure to tip the gate first before he came back to ask her if she was OK, because he was a gentleman but he wasn't certain that she was above pretending to fall just to secure a sneaky victory.

CHAPTER 34

'Did you hear they got the fellows who were doing those burglaries?' Lilac's mum said over dinner, as if this was something of very little importance.

'Really?' Gerry replied through a mouthful of spinach-from-the-garden, which took lot of chewing. He didn't sound particularly interested.

'WHAT?' Lilac swallowed her bite of fish finger in double time. 'What "fellows"? Who was it? Was it the man in the cap?'

'What man in the cap, Lilac? Don't bolt your food like that, you'll choke. It was someone who'd been going round pretending to be a builder, asking to be let into houses to see the roof of the house next door. He'd scope out the place, see if there was anything worth taking, and come back that night with a friend. Marguerite McDonagh at the tennis club told me all about it. They even got her jewellery back. She's none too pleased; she was hoping the insurance would be enough for a holiday.'

Lilac went pink. 'He came to our door. I nearly let him

in, but Guzzler growled. Maybe Man in Cap is the accomplice. That must be it.'

'Did he? Good for Guzzler, he always knows.' Nuala didn't seem particularly perturbed by their narrow escape. 'But who is this Man in Cap you're talking about, Lilac?'

'The man I kept seeing. He's the thief, I'm sure he is.' Lilac described Cap Man to her parents.

Gerry knitted his brows. 'Hmm . . . that does sound familiar. Can't put my finger on it, but I have a feeling I know who you're talking about.'

'Oh, Dad, think harder. I have to know who he is, so we can tell the police and they can catch the accomplice.'

'No, Lilac,' Nuala said patiently, 'they got both the people who were doing it. There's nobody else to catch.'

'But maybe they're innocent! Maybe it's a terrible miscarriage of justice!'

'They recovered the stolen goods. The two of them told the Guards how they did it. I got the whole story from Marguerite McDonagh, because her Shane's wife's sister works at the Garda station. There's no more to the story, Lilac, I promise. I'm sorry if your detective skills didn't uncover the truth, but maybe there'll be a new mystery to solve soon.'

'Fine, Mum, no need to be sarky.' Lilac grumpily returned her attention to her dinner.

'So, did your dad get his missing heirloom back, then?' Lilac asked Michael next time she saw him, which was the next day passing by the playground. She'd taken Guzzler for a walk, and Michael seemed to be supervising Jimmy playing in the sandpit, which was unusual. It was breezy and almost, but not quite, drizzling.

'No. Why?'

'Because they caught the burglars. And people got their stuff back. And it wasn't Cap Man at all,' Lilac said downheartedly.

'Oh. I didn't hear that. But I don't think we were actually burgled. Jimmy's been taking our stuff and burying it all over the place. He says my headphones are in the sandpit. Keep digging!' he added as an aside to Jimmy, who was digging like mad but coming up empty-shovelled.

'What? Really? Jimmy, why would you do that?' Lilac said sternly, feeling it was her duty as one of his elders and betters to give out to him.

Pretty much everyone he knew had already given out to Jimmy, and the only way things could get worse was if he was actually arrested, he thought, so he was trying very hard to dig back up the things he had taken. He was confident that he hadn't stolen them, he'd just moved them. It was hard to explain all that, though, so he shrugged and said miserably, 'I dunno.'

'Mum says it's a cry for attention. She thinks David and I need to spend more time with him.' Michael didn't sound like he agreed, but here he was with Jimmy, so maybe it was working.

'But then' – Lilac's brain was ticking like a time-bomb – 'maybe the box I found is your dad's after all. Jimmy, did you take a silver box out of your dad's desk and bury it on the beach?'

'Nope,' said Jimmy very quickly without looking up.

'Jimmy, you have to tell us. You won't get into trouble,'

Michael said. 'Well, you might, but you're already in trouble. You may as well get it over with.' He felt compelled to be honest about it.

'No. I didn't.' Jimmy still wouldn't look up and Lilac even thought he might be crying, though that didn't seem like a very Jimmy thing to do. Usually, Jimmy was hard as nails. She'd seen him take a flyer off his skateboard – well, David's skateboard actually – and come up with two badly grazed knees and just run off as if nothing had happened.

The little shovel caught on something and Jimmy scraped at it quickly to reveal a thin black wire that soon led to the rest of Michael's headphones. The spongy bits over the earpieces were full of sand, but otherwise they looked unaffected.

'Well, that's something. I hope they still work.' Michael put on his sternest voice, but was relieved that at least now they could go home. He even felt a little bad for Jimmy, getting himself into all this hot water just because everyone ignored him. Michael wouldn't have minded being ignored a bit more often, he thought. He'd be able to get away with all sorts of things.

'I have the box still,' Lilac said as they headed up the road. 'I didn't bring it back to the Garda station yet. I sort of, um, lost the form they gave me, so I was waiting to get another one. We can show it to your dad and see what he says.'

Jimmy burst into loud, snotty tears. Lilac and Michael exchanged a look of exasperation, and Lilac hunkered down to be on a level with Jimmy's face. It was a wet, pink, scrunched-up mess. 'Jimmy,' she said more gently than before. 'What is it? We know you took the things, and we have the box and it's not damaged, so why is this worse? Your dad will be happy to get it back.'

'Dad told me not to tell about the box. He said it's important not to. I don't know why, but he doesn't want anyone to bring it back.' It took three goes for Lilac to understand what Jimmy was saying, between the heaves and the sobs and the massive sniffles to get the river of snot under control.

'Well that makes no sense at all,' Lilac said briskly to Michael, straightening up. 'I'm going to get the box. Of course your dad wants it back. It's an heirloom. And it has his cigarettes in it . . . oh, it did, until I threw them out.'

'My dad doesn't smoke, though. Maybe those were just really old cigarettes. From the time of the inscription, like.'

'Oh, I hope I didn't throw away historical-artefact cigarettes.'

'I was joking. At least, I think I was.'

'Oh, right. Sorry. Anyway, wait here.'

Michael stood awkwardly outside Lilac's house while she ran upstairs. Jimmy wiped his nose on the back of his sleeve and sniffled so hard and wetly that Michael almost gagged. A minute later, Lilac reappeared, box in hand.

'Is your dad at home?'

'Yes, he's watching the golf.'

Mr Jennings was in the front room, leaning forward in his armchair so that his nose almost touched the television screen, murmuring 'Get it in for the bogey, go on go on, Seve, ya good thing.' He didn't look happy to be disturbed, but once the little white ball had disappeared into the hole and everyone seemed pleased with the result, he looked up to see what it was his sons and their young friend were trying to tell him. His eyes lit on the box, but his expression was not one of perfect delight to see it restored to him.

'That's my – I mean, what's that you've got there?'

'It's your box you lost, isn't it, Dad?'

'Well, now, I don't know. It *might* be . . .' Mr Jennings reached out to take it from Lilac, but she held it back. 'Wait, this will tell you for sure . . .' she said.

'Don't open it!' he said as if in panic, but she had already flipped up the lid and was turning it around to show him the inscription.

'Oh!' He sounded oddly relieved. 'Ah. Yes. To Fred from Avril. My goodness. It is my one. Fred was my grandfather, though I always thought my grandmother's name was Betty, not Avril. I'd forgotten about that engraving. Hah!'

Mrs Jennings came into the room asking incomprehensibly, 'Did Seve get down in two, or does the eejit in the knickerbockers have it?' but then she noticed the children and looked inquiringly at them. 'Oh, Lilac, hello. Jimmy, my goodness, what's wrong?' Jimmy was still standing at the back, sniffling.

'I found Mr Jennings's box!' Lilac declared. 'Guzzler found it on the beach. Though I'm sorry, I threw away the cigarettes, Mr Jennings.'

'Cigarettes? What cigarettes?' Mrs Jennings said, looking up quickly with her eyes narrowed, the way Guzzler did when he was trying to figure out if someone had been frying rashers an hour earlier while he was in the garden.

'Oh, nothing, darling! Nothing at all.' Mr Jennings frowned at Michael and Lilac and seemed to be trying to send semaphore signals with his eyebrows. Lilac divined that his eyebrows were saying 'Whatever you do, don't mention the cigarettes.'

'Sorry, nothing, never mind,' she said quickly, impressed by her own smartness. 'So anyway, it was on the beach, Guzzler found it a while ago.' She launched into the story of how Gerry had taken it to Mr Byrne's and how interesting the inscription was, to distract from the issue of the cigarettes, which appeared somehow to be a touchy subject.

'That is an interesting inscription, all right. I seem to remember asking my mother about it years ago, but for some reason she didn't want to even look at it. Well, thank you very much, Lilac, for finding it, and Jimmy, you needn't worry, you're not in worse trouble. Just see if you can dig up David's missing articles now and we'll call it a day. They're teeing up for the next hole, off you all go.' And he returned his attention to the fairways and water hazards of the small screen.

CHAPTER 35

'Lilac.' Gerry nudged her as they walked to Mass on Sunday morning. He pointed to a lamppost.

'What, Dad? Don't bump me like that.' She distanced herself from him a little. You couldn't be seen walking too close to your father in public, as if you liked his company or something.

'Is that your man in the cap, by any chance?'

'Where?'

'Up there. On the poster.'

Lilac looked up. There were election posters on all the lampposts in the town, and one in particular was very eye-catching with its red-and-white lettering and a big photo of a smiling youngish man . . . in a tweed cap.

'That's him! What's he doing on a poster?'

'He's running for election, of course. He's the local candidate. He's been chatting up people all over town for ages now, the way politicians do, smiling and calling you by your name and holding babies and patting dogs. The posters have been up for a while. I'm surprised you didn't notice.'

'Oh. Right. It's not that I didn't *notice* the posters,' she tried to explain, 'it's just that I put them in a separate part of my brain from the part that was looking for Cap Man.' Lilac sighed. 'I'm a terrible detective. You're right, I don't notice anything.'

Lilac was still thinking about the conversation she'd had with Jeannie the night before, when she'd come to babysit. Jeannie said she and David had broken up.

'Oh no! I'm sorry.' Lilac knew breaking up was a terrible thing. 'Do you need lots of ice cream or something? Is your heart broken? Will you never love again?'

'No, it's not like that. It's fine, really. I mean, the kissing was nice, but we're fine as friends.'

'Really? It's just . . . OK? Do you hate him?'

'No. He got train tracks and he was really self-conscious about them. And he has to study for his exams. And we didn't really have conversations, as such, when we were on our own. That's why we were kissing instead.'

'So did he break up with you or did you break up with him?'

'He said it, but I was thinking it too.'

'Well, that's lucky.'

'Yep. Are we watching *The Fall Guy* or is it *The A-Team* tonight? Are there any chocolate biscuits?'

'Sure. I like Face better than Howie. Let's watch *The A-Team*.'

Life continued to be not what Lilac was expecting. She sort of liked that about it.

CHAPTER 36

Dear Margery,

I told you all about how the box was Mr Jennings's heirloom thingy after all, didn't I? I don't know why I didn't think of that as soon as Michael told me they were missing something, but he never actually said it was a silver box, so I didn't. But there was more to the story, and it was very tragic and romantic and also bonkers. This is what Michael told me really happened, after he asked his Granny about it.

They went to see their granny on Sunday and Michael thought it would be interesting to bring the box and ask her about the inscription. The Granny (who I am going to call The Granny because she's not my Granny) can be grumpy and it gets awkward trying to chat, so he says it's good to have something prepared to talk about.

He took the box out and he said that the silver marks showed that it was made in Birmingham in 1907, and did she know that? And The Granny was even grumpier than usual and snapped his head off and left the room. But then about five minutes later she came back in and offered him a custard cream, and smiled at him, and she looked about 75 instead of 105 the way she usually looks. And then she told him the whole story while he ate all the custard creams and she didn't even stop him.

So the first time The Granny had ever seen the box was when they were clearing out after her parents died, years and years ago (obviously), when Mr Jennings her son (Michael's dad) was about 25. And he found the box in a drawer and showed her the inscription, just like we did, and she saw it and was concerned, because she didn't know who Avril was. And she thought it meant that her father had had an affair, and that her parents' happy marriage hadn't been happy after all. And she was very upset, as someone would be, and she sort of took it out on Mr Jennings her son (not Mr Jennings her husband) because if he hadn't shown it to her, she'd never have known about it. (Which of course is silly, but Mum says people do things like that. It's called shooting the messenger.)

So of course she wasn't happy to see the box again when Michael showed it to her. But after she'd left the room she thought about what he'd said and she realised that her parents hadn't met until her father came to Ireland from England in 1914 (something to do with the war). So if the box was made in 1907, that was from much earlier in his life — because nobody engraves an old box, they do it when it's new, like our blackboard duster for Miss Grey. And she remembered that he had been engaged a long time earlier to a girl who died tragically (of course), and she realised <u>that</u> must have been Avril.

So the box didn't mean that The Granny's father had been a dirty rotten low-down lying cheater after all, and after all those years of shooting the messenger — I mean, being horrible to Mr-Jennings-her-son and his kids — The Granny could start being nice to them again.

I know I shouldn't say bad things about old people, but some old people are bonkers. The Granny even apologised for making David and Michael take terrible confirmation names, but it's not like they can go back in time and change them. I suppose Jimmy won't have to have one, so that's something nice for Jimmy.

And now that Jeannie and David have broken up, David doesn't even care if Jimmy ever digs up the earrings he buried or not.

So even if I didn't manage to detect anything at all with the burglaries and Cap Man, at least the Mystery of the Silver Box, that I didn't even know was a mystery, ended happily.

Love from your historical drama expert, Lilac

CHAPTER 37

The excitement of the last day of school was totally overshadowed for most of Lilac's class by the much bigger excitement of Miss Grey's wedding, the day after that. Even though they were all busy cleaning the classroom – stacking the tables and chairs against the radiators, sweeping the floor so it could be polished over the break, tackling the most horrible task of cleaning the enormous venetian blinds, one sharp flippy slat at a time – the usual feeling of it being the last day they would see each other for months and months was missing.

Several of the girls would see each other again the next day: at the church, where they would finally find out what Miss Grey's dress looked like, what colour her bridesmaids were wearing, and whether she was carrying carnations or roses. They would also, of course, present Miss Grey with her gift from the class. Lilac had already collected it and wrapped it in paper approved by at least seven classmates, all of whom had crowded into the newsagent's after school on Wednesday to contemplate the paltry selection of options available there. (There were only two designated 'wedding' wrapping papers – a pink one with kittens and horseshoes and 'Congratulations!' banners, and a blue one with puppies and horseshoes and 'Congratulations!' banners. Instead of either, they chose a tasteful silver swirly pattern that could be reused for other purposes. 'A christening present!' Agatha said with glee.)

Lilac was not so happy about being the official minder of the rest of the class-owned roll of wrapping paper, because she wasn't sure how she'd keep it safely unused, but she agreed that she could clearly label it to make sure it didn't go astray. As the sole only child in the class, she agreed that she probably had a less chaotic household than anyone else. At least in Lilac's house, if you put something away, you could usually rely on it to still be there when you went looking for it. So long as you remembered where it was. Everyone else had annoying big brothers with no respect for property, sisters who would 'borrow' your stuff, or little siblings who were nothing but mobile agents of destruction. Not to mention mothers who would go on unpredictable cleaning binges and throw random things away without even asking. Lilac's mother was not prone to cleaning binges.

So at the end of the half day, they all went home saying 'See you tomorrow' instead of the usual, gleeful 'See you in September', and it almost didn't feel like the start of the summer holidays at all.

'Lilac,' said her mother the next morning, 'I don't have to tell you this, do I?'

'No, probably not,' said Lilac cheekily. 'But you're going to, aren't you? What is it?'

'Just to be very, extremely, *supremely* quiet and respectful at the church. Remember, this is Miss Grey's big day, and you girls aren't really even supposed to be there. So you have to creep in and sit quietly like mice at the very back, and then give her the present afterwards, outside, when she's finished talking to all her important guests. And generally not make a show of yourselves,' Nuala finished up, wondering if she was demanding the impossible of a classful of hyped-up girls. 'I'd go with you myself to keep order, except that I think the fewer uninvited people there the better. It would be rude to just arrive looking like I was there out of nosiness.'

'But lots of other people go to weddings just out of nosiness,' Lilac pointed out. 'Or sometimes you're passing the church when there's a wedding on and you hang around to catch a glimpse. Angela Delaney says her granny goes up to the church every Saturday afternoon in the summer to see who's getting married and what they look like. It's her hobby. It's good for an older person to keep active, you know.'

'Yes. Indeed.' Lilac could see that Nuala disapproved of Angela Delaney's granny but didn't want to say so. 'Well, anyway, I have things to do here, so I can't go with you. Just make sure the girls all know how important it is. No giggling or whispering at the back. In fact, maybe it would be best if you just stayed outside the church and waited for it to be all over.'

'Mu-um! No way! I want to see her walk up the aisle, and the moment when she takes her veil off and the first kiss and all those important things.'

'Well, you know, it's just a Mass, with extra bits. It can be quite boring, to be honest. And long. Some wedding ceremonies are very long.' Nuala spoke as if she'd experienced one long wedding too many.

'Mum. It'll be fine. We'll all be very good. I promise.'

Three in the afternoon took forever to arrive. Lilac spent a good hour deciding what to wear, because she wanted to strike a perfect balance between dressed up enough and not dressed up too much, since she wasn't actually going to the party after the church part of the wedding. It all came down to accessories, since she only had one good outfit (the purple Sodastream syrup had never really come out of the apple-green dress she wore on her Confirmation day, so it was her blue-and-white birthday party dress). She decided to dress it down by wearing ankle socks and light, thin-soled runners, and a summery yellow cardigan instead of a white one. She rummaged through her mother's bag collection to find something big enough to carry the present in that would look a little nicer than a plastic bag from Penney's, and was pleased to unearth a large greyish-blue canvas shoulder bag that might go quite well.

Eventually it was time to go and call for Agatha. They had decided to go together, because – well, no matter how much they felt entitled to be there as members of Miss Grey's class, there was still an element of safety in numbers.

As they got closer to the church, Lilac detected something a little like butterflies in her tummy. She asked

Agatha, 'Did your mum tell you to be extra super-duper good?'

'Of course she did.'

'Do you think everyone's mums did?'

'Probably.'

'I'm a bit worried, though, that it'll be hard for us all to be as good as we should be. Even if we're trying very hard.'

'So am I.'

'Because it would be really really awful to mess up the wedding.'

'I know.'

For a moment they both felt like turning around and pretending they'd never intended to go to the wedding, but they had responsibilities. For one thing, they were already dressed up. For another, Lilac was carrying the present, which had to be given to Miss Grey. She'd be gone on her honeymoon after today and nobody would see her again till school started in September.

Their footsteps slowed down a bit, though, the closer they got to the church. At the gate, Lilac looked around, puzzled. 'Shouldn't there be more people here? Where are all the cars?' One red car was driving out, but otherwise the car park looked no more full than on a normal Saturday afternoon when a few people used it while they did their shopping.

'Maybe everyone walked to the wedding?' Agatha said doubtfully. Then she brightened up. 'There's Katie. And Maura Rooney.' They watched the two girls come around from the other side of the building. Katie was shaking her head mournfully. For a terrible moment, Lilac thought maybe the wedding had been called off.

'He didn't leave her at the altar, did he? Or turn out to be already married to a madwoman who lives in his attic? Or . . .' She couldn't think of any other reasons why a wedding wouldn't go ahead as planned. There were tiny bits of confetti on the ground at her feet, and she spotted a lonely pink carnation outside the main door of the church.

'No, it's worse than that! They've gone already! It was at one o'clock, not three like we thought.'

'Oh, phew. That's not worse, Katie. At least, only for us. Not for them.'

'Here come the others.' Adele Duffy, Laura Devine and Rachel Jackson were just coming in at the gate, and the two Jennys could be seen in the distance across the car park, where the pedestrian entrance was. The news was passed around dolefully.

'Well, we'll just have to take the show on the road,' said Adele, who was never despondent for long.

'Uh, what?' asked Laura.

'I mean, we'll have to go to the reception and give her the present there. Obviously.'

'But we don't know where it is,' Agatha said.

'I do. It's at the Park Hotel. My mum heard about it.' Rachel Jackson was surprisingly informative.

'Ooh, posh,' said several people at once. The Park even had a swimming pool.

'How are we going to get there?'

CHAPTER 38

'I have an idea,' said Adele. 'Follow me.' She led the way out of the church car park and up the lane by its side, to the Garda station.

'Why are we going to the Garda station?' Lilac asked, voicing the thoughts of many.

'My brother's a guard. He just graduated from Templemore last month and they sent him here.'

'And he's going to fly us to the Park in his Garda helicopter?' said Katie sarcastically.

'No. But he might be able to give us a lift, if we say it's an emergency.'

They all pushed the heavy door open and crowded into the small room in front of the window. Adele didn't bother with the bell; she just shouted.

'Aengus! Aengus!'

The young guard Lilac and Agatha had encountered came out of the side room, eating an apple. He took the sight of a gaggle of eleven-year-old girls in his stride, and paused for another bite before asking his sister what she needed.

'We need a lift! We have to give our teacher her wedding present, and you're the only one who can get us there. You have to save the day!' Adele said urgently. Then she looked at the girls. 'Aengus loves saving the day. That's why he's a guard. The fire brigade was full up or he'd have done that.'

Aengus looked at his apple core, inspecting it for further potential. Then he took careful aim at the bin under the desk and pot-shotted it in. He looked up with a grin.

'Right then. Out the back with yiz.' He opened the door beside the window-to-talk-through, ushered the girls into the big room and past all the desks with their unattended paperwork, and opened the door at the end. This led to the area where the guards parked their cars, noses out and ready to speed off to chase down bank robbers at a moment's notice.

'Two in the front, four on the back seat and three on the laps,' he said briskly, assessing the situation. 'Or five and two – no childbearing hips on you lot yet. Go on, get in, it's a big car.'

It was a big car. It lacked the extra hatchback space of Lilac's dad's car, but it was much roomier across the back seat, so there really was room for five – or four and a half; Maura was sitting sideways, half on the seat and half on the door handle. The window winder was sticking into her side, but she didn't say a word. Adele sat in the front, as sister of the driver, but her pride of place was somewhat marred by having Rachel Jackson on her knee. They carefully stretched the seatbelt around them both and clicked it into place.

'Why am I always on someone's knee?' wailed Agatha.

'My head's squashed against the ceiling.'

'Because you're the smallest,' Lilac said reasonably as she tried to put her elbows somewhere out of the way of everyone else's elbows. 'All our heads would be squashed even more. At least nobody's squeezing the breath out of you. Can you move forward a bit so you're not sitting on my tummy?'

'Grand so,' said Aengus the Guard, imperturbably surveying the scene through the car windows. 'We'll only be on the road a minute, sure.' It was true that the Park Hotel was local, but a minute might be pushing it. Lilac was sure it was closer to ten, or they would have just walked there. Aengus sat into the driver's seat, clicked his seatbelt officiously, and flicked on his indicator to pull out.

They moved off smoothly. There must be some sort of cast-iron suspension in Garda cars, Lilac thought, because she was sure the bottom would scrape the kerb as they drove away, but the grinding screech never came. She wanted to duck her head down out of sight, but she didn't have enough space to do that. Here I am, mortified again, she thought to herself. Then, all at once, she decided she was finished with being embarrassed by the ridiculous situations life kept putting her in. Instead of blushing and hiding, she grinned and looked around happily, for once enjoying the funny side while it happened instead of two weeks afterwards.

As they left they passed another car on the way in – driven by the same red-faced older guard that Lilac's birthday party had encountered. 'I think he might explode,' Adele observed, as they all waved at him from their respective windows. He did seem even more red in the face than usual, but Aengus just said, 'Ah, he'll be grand. He needs to take his blood pressure pills, that's all.'

'Are you going to turn on the nee-naw?' Jenny Kelly asked. She was bouncing up and down on Theresa with great excitement, but Theresa was sturdy enough to take it without wincing. Not too much, anyway.

'I am not,' Aengus replied with dignity, and that was that.

Six and a half minutes later they opened the doors and all but fell out of the car in the resplendent yellow-gravel driveway of the Park Hotel. Aengus hadn't turned on the siren, but Lilac suspected he'd broken the speed limit just the same. 'Is this what being born feels like?' Agatha asked as she emerged, for added melodrama. Nobody answered her, because that was an icky thought.

They thanked Aengus, flexed their stiff joints, straightened their skirts, and made sure Lilac still had the present. 'It's just as well we never got that giant card. It would never have survived the crush,' Katie O pointed out. Even though it was true, nobody agreed with her. They'd really wanted the giant one, and there was some lingering bad feeling about how she hadn't really made an effort. She had been in charge of the card, and had ended up buying quite a modest-sized one because she said she couldn't get to the shop in town that had the giant ones.

Together, the nine girls walked up the impressive front steps of the hotel and hesitantly into the lobby. Lilac thought the best thing to do would be to continue straight ahead as if they knew exactly where they were going, and work it out as they went along, but Theresa strode up to the woman behind the desk, who was giving them all the stink-eye.

'We're here for Miss Grey's wedding,' Theresa said confidently. Lilac was impressed. Agatha moved herself surreptitiously to the back of the group, certain they were going to be thrown out any second now when they failed to produce invitations. But the woman decided they looked respectable enough and said pleasantly, 'The Magillicuddy Suite, through those doors to the right and down at the end of the hall. But I think they're out the back taking photos before the rain starts. You can go that way, it's quicker.' She nodded at the central doorway and smiled.

The girls paused in front of the doors. Outside, they could see nicely dressed people in twos and threes and bigger groups, chatting quietly or laughing uproariously, everyone holding a glass of what was probably champagne. In the middle of the rose garden were Miss Grey and her new husband – and Lilac was suddenly a little overwhelmed by the thought of a husband: Jeannie and David came to her mind, and Michael's grandmother's parents and Avril who had died, and Lilac's own parents; they all tumbled together there in a whirlwind of couples who were happy or sad or ill-fated or just married. How did this love thing work, she wondered, fleetingly. How could you possibly be sure enough to marry someone?

And there they were – the newest, happiest, surest couple – being ordered into awkward-looking poses by a photographer who evidently took his job very seriously. There was a cluster of bridesmaids off to the right, in long peach-coloured satin dresses with flounces and ruffles everywhere one would fit, and a few more places besides.

'Oh, it's just beautiful,' Agatha breathed. For once,

nobody accused her of being too romantic. They all realised at the same moment that this was exactly the wedding of their dreams, every last ruffle of it.

CHAPTER 39

And then Maura Rooney pushed the door open and the girls advanced, just as the dark clouds overhead that had been nowhere in sight a minute earlier began to release fat raindrops, in ones and twos, splashing in people's drinks and making the bridesmaids shriek about their hair. The guests began to move towards the doors at the other end of the building, which evidently led into the Magillicuddy Suite, but there was some confusion there because people were coming out at the same time. A group of boys ran through the crowd in the direction of the rose garden, where the bridesmaids were now trying to untangle the bride's dress from the thorns it had caught on while attempting some ill-fated pose for the camera.

'That's Michael!' said Lilac. 'How is he here?'

'Your friend Michael from the boys' school? Maybe the fiancé is his teacher. I heard he works there,' Rachel supplied; she was a fount of knowledge today.

'What? No! His teacher's old and grumpy.'

'Grumpy people get married too.'

'Sarky.'

'Lads, we have to give her the present, remember?' Theresa, of all people, was the voice of reason. The rain was getting heavier, after all. They reached the rose garden at the same time as the boys, who looked suspiciously as if they were on a similar mission. Michael was holding something wrapped in blue horseshoes-and-puppies paper, and one of the other boys carried a giant envelope that he couldn't possibly keep out of the rain.

Lilac didn't really want to be the one to do it, but she was carrying the gift, so she had to. And she wasn't going to be embarrassed any more, so she just went ahead. The others stopped and let her step forward, and just as Miss Grey – who was presumably Miss Grey no longer – finally released herself from the rosebush and looked up to see what the hullaballoo was, Lilac held out the package and the card and said, as rehearsed: 'Miss Grey, we got you something from the class to remember your special day by. Happy . . . wedding.' She hadn't been meant to say that last part, but she felt it needed something more.

Miss Grey looked slightly dazed by the sudden appearance of half her class, because she had thought school was over and done with until September and now suddenly here were some children who were probably about to demand instruction on decimals or the dates of the Iron Age. She collected herself, took the present graciously, thanked the girls, and said that they'd all better go in before they got soaked.

Michael and his friends seemed to have handed over their burden at the same time, as Miss Grey's brand-new husband was also holding his gift, and everyone made a run for it just as the heavens really opened.

'Happens at every wedding, you know,' commented an elderly man, waving Lilac in ahead of him. He was wearing a festive yellow tie and a waterproof fisherman's hat and seemed quite happy about it all, though that might have been thanks to the glass of sherry he was holding. 'I've seen them all. Either there's a hurricane blowing the whole time or it pours just as they start the photos. There hasn't been a dry June Saturday in decades. Bottoms up!' He drained his glass. Lilac stared at him, remembering a piece of paper pinned to the front of her uniform one day in the classroom.

'Are you Uncle John?' she asked.

'I am indeed. Are you one of my great-nieces?'

'No, no, it's just the weather and the sherry . . . oh, never mind, nice to meet you.'

The bridesmaids' peach satin dresses were turning a little see-through now that they were wet, but their wearers didn't seem to have noticed. Miss Grey's hair had somehow been caught in the rose bush too, and half of it had fallen out of its elegant French roll and was flopping over to one side. Her groom was being grumpy at Michael and the other boys, so Lilac assumed he was indeed the Mr O'Grady she had heard about – though he didn't look anything like as old as she'd imagined. She watched him open his parcel and extract something that looked oddly like a well-worn tweed jacket with shiny new leather elbow patches. He seemed happier. Manly handshakes were exchanged and the boys were smiling now.

Miss Grey's high heels seemed to be giving her some trouble. She sat down at one of the tables that were set for dinner and eased her feet out of them, mostly hidden under the long tablecloth. The girls crowded around her saying, 'Go on, Miss Grey, open it, open it.' Agatha asked 'Did you have a lovely ceremony?' but nobody heard her. Miss Grey fumbled with the silver paper and finally tore it off to reveal the blackboard duster in all its spanking-new glory, shiny-smooth yellow and soft fluffy black. 'Read the inscription,' they all demanded. She held it up so that the sunlight that was now making the wet garden glimmer reflected off the little bronze plaque, and read aloud:

To Miss Grey from your Not Tupperware class

'Oh girls. It's lovely. I'll use it every day and think of you.'

They all nudged each other. 'See? See? We knew you would.'

'That's why we chose it.'

'It was my idea.'

'No it wasn't.'

'Well, it was sort of all of ours.'

'Do you like it?'

'She just said she did.'

'I love it, really and truly, I do.' Miss Grey smiled the smile of a bride who can finally start to relax because the rain has come down but the day hasn't been ruined.

The girls beamed with delight, and a waiter came over with a tray of sandwiches just for them, even though they hadn't been invited at all.

THE END

ACKNOWLEDGEMENTS

A big thank you goes out to my beta readers, Caoimhe Naessens, Ciara Daly, Elissa Mara and Millie McCarthy. Thanks are also due (again) to Emily Rainsford Ryan for the cover illustration and Suzy Hastings for the cover design. And thanks to my family, for being my biggest fans – and to the newcomers, Oak and Birch, for not sitting on the keyboard any more than was absolutely necessary.

ABOUT THE AUTHOR

Christine Doran grew up in Dublin, Ireland. At the age of twenty-nine and a half she moved to the United States, where she now lives with her husband, her children, and two rambunctious cats. Lilac in Scarlet is her second novel.

To find out more about Lilac's world and to keep up to date with her further adventures, go to

www.lilacthegirl.blogspot.com

Lilac will return in *Lilac Blue,* coming soon.

Printed in Great Britain
by Amazon

14257416R00118